GABRIEL'S TRUMPET

GABRIEL'S TRUMPET

Robert Don Hughes

Broadman & Holman Publishers

Nashville, Tennessee

© Copyright 1993
BROADMAN & HOLMAN PUBLISHERS
All Rights Reserved

4260-59

ISBN: 0-8054-6059-4

Dewey Decimal Classification: Juvenile Fiction
Subject Heading: Christian Life—Fiction
Library of Congress Card Catalog Number: 92-47267

Printed in the United States of America

Library of Congress Cataloging-in-Publication Data:
Hughes, Robert Don, 1949-
  Gabriel's Trumpet / Robert Don Hughes.
   p. cm.
   ISBN: 0-8054-6059-4
   PZ7.H87385Qu 1993
   [Fic]—dc20   92-47267
                                                     CIP
                                                     AC

FOR YOU, DAD
You would have loved it, just because I wrote it.
See you in the morning.

Contents

1. Polishing 1
2. The Trumpet of Doom 9
3. Who Will Go? 17
4. On the Road 28
5. Emerald Green 35
6. The Rescue of Leffingwell 40
7. Riding Blind 46
8. In the Rebel Camp 55
9. Left Behind 63
10. Lucifer's Pavilion 71
11. Abandoned 83
12. Forgiveness 92
13. One Last Supper 99
14. The Darkest Hour 106
15. Jack's Jump 119
16. King's Knight 128

I

Polishing

Eric hated polishing armor.

He hadn't always felt that way. When he'd finally been made a squire, he'd taken great pride in buffing a painted shield until it reflected like a mirror. On tournament day he would watch as the knights came hurtling together, realizing with a thrill that they both glistened in the sunlight because of his expert shine.

Now, when he heard the clank of spear-point and the splintering of a wooden lance, all Eric could think was, *There's another breastplate I'll have to polish tonight.* Sure enough, by afternoon a slightly-damaged breastplate would be added to his pile.

He peered at himself in the sword he'd just polished to a cold, hard gleam. The face that looked back at him didn't please him at all. The eyes were not the piercing, valiant blue of a warrior. They were a muddy gray. His hair was neither golden blond nor stark, handsome black. It was just a dirty light brown, and it constantly hung in his eyes. He thought briefly of grabbing his bangs and sawing them off with this blade—but he thought better of it. Eric was a cautious sort. He tried not to do anything impulsively. He tucked the blade under his arm to polish the jeweled pommel.

Eric never volunteered for this duty. It got dumped on him because, at thirteen, he was the youngest, smallest squire in the barracks. The older boys—bullies, most of them, in Eric's opinion—couldn't be bothered to buff and polish the plate-armor of their own masters. And why should they when young Eric was so good at it—and so pliable? He loathed the fact that they all thought of him that way.

To be honest, Eric knew it wasn't the work itself he hated. He considered himself the most dependable of all the squires he knew. He worked at it. That's why he'd advanced so quickly to this lofty level of the King's service—because those who had watched him grow believed him capable of most anything. Some days that made him feel good about himself. Other days, like today, he despised himself for allowing the older squires to take advantage of him.

"One of these days," he murmured to the sword, "I'm going to tell them all just what they can do with their armor!"

"And what would that be?" demanded Lawrence as he stepped through the open doorway into the stable. Eric shivered and tried to make himself smaller. Lawrence was one of three nineteen-year-old squires in this division. Powerfully built, he seemed particularly in love with himself. He wore a malicious smile as he stalked through the hay to tower over Eric. "Why not tell me now?" He smirked as he thrust a dull helmet into Eric's face, daring the younger boy to act on his resolve.

Eric gazed up at Lawrence, his jaw tight. "You can—," he began furiously, but his courage faltered. He knew Lawrence would beat him up. "You can put it over there," he sighed, "on the pile."

"Oh, no," Lawrence snarled, stooping to stick his nose in Eric's face. "I'm going to put it in your lap, and you're going to have it done before you get up from there! My master's off on a quest tomorrow morning, and he can't depart with a dirty helmet—now, can he?"

Eric squirmed in discomfort. He didn't like Lawrence standing this close to him, and Lawrence knew it. "Where's he going?"

he mumbled, hoping a change of subject would get his oppressor out of his face. "I haven't heard anything about any quest."

"Of course not," the larger boy snorted. "Who'd tell anything to an insect like you?" Eric managed to stomach the contemptuous tone of voice because, at last, Lawrence straightened up and stepped away. "He's going on a special assignment for the King."

Eric picked the helmet up out of his lap and studied it. He could finish it in minutes. So could Lawrence, for that matter, if he would take his obligations seriously. "Where?"

"I'm not telling you," Lawrence sneered.

"Do you even know?" said Eric, mimicking the other boy's surly manner. Suddenly he felt himself being jerked up out of the straw by the shoulders.

"Just what do you mean by that?" Lawrence shouted, literally spitting in his face. Eric felt his feet dangling inches over the straw, smelled his captor's stinking breath, and arrived calmly at the realization that he was, indeed, going to get pounded. That freed him, somehow. After all, he had not tried to antagonize Lawrence. If the older squire wanted to make him the target for all his frustrations, there was little Eric could do about it. Acknowledging his helplessness, Eric no longer flinched. He gazed into Lawrence's glittering eyes and responded:

"I'm saying that you're still a squire, Lawrence, and they don't tell squires anything we don't have to know."

Lawrence's face turned red with rage. Eric had touched on the single most infuriating fact of Lawrence's life—old as he was, he was still a squire. He had not yet been dubbed a knight, and he was certain that behind his back the whole city wondered why. Eric knew, of course. It was behavior like this that mired Lawrence in the ranks of the "not-quite" men. His childish rage, coupled with his full-grown strength, rendered him brutal, while knights were gentle and unselfish. He was also foolish where knights were wise. Eric saw these things clearly. He wondered why Lawrence didn't see them.

At the moment Lawrence saw nothing but red. He lifted Eric still farther off the straw with one hand and drew back his fist to strike, roaring rather than speaking his response. At that precise moment, Jack Lackin stuck his head into the stables.

"Hello, men," he smiled cheerfully, but his knowing eyes took in the whole situation at a glance.

Lawrence immediately dropped his victim and whirled around to face the intruder. Eric sprawled backward onto the straw, saved momentarily from the older boy's bludgeoning fists. Odd—he felt strangely disappointed.

"What do you want?" Lawrence thundered at the grinning garbageman.

"Just checking for trash," Jack Lackin shrugged. "Any in here?"

"Why don't you keep your nose out of other people's business?" Lawrence snarled, but he also started out of the stables. Eric marked that carefully, for while the trashman was no bigger than his nemesis, certainly, neither was Jack only half his size. Knights were also courageous, Eric reminded himself. Did Lawrence lack the courage even to face the garbage collector?

"Oh, you won't want to forget this," Jack added as Lawrence shuffled by him, and he stooped to retrieve the dull helmet Lawrence had brought for Eric to polish. In the excitement Eric hadn't even realized he'd dropped it. Now Jack gave it a quick rub with his full sleeve and handed the helmet back to Lawrence. "Since he's leaving in the morning, your master will probably need you to polish this."

Lawrence glared at Jack Lackin, then jerked the helmet away. "You know, Lackinsense," Lawrence snarled, using a nickname freely applied to the trashman throughout the city, "I wonder why I didn't smell you coming! You stink!"

Jack Lackin's cheerful visage never altered. "That's an occupational hazard," he chuckled. "Fact is, nobody else cares to clean up the messes around here. While it's a dirty job, somebody does have to do it!"

"Fitting that it should be you," Lawrence sneered, some of his arrogance returning. "You're nothing but garbage yourself!" Tucking the helmet under his arm, Lawrence strolled out into the afternoon sunlight.

Jack Lackin turned his head to smile after him, then looked back down at Eric. "Need some help?" he asked quietly.

"I'm fine," Eric mumbled, climbing to his feet and shaking the straw from the back of his tunic. "He didn't really mean all that," he added, concerned about the trashman's feelings.

"Oh, but he did!" Jack Lackin smiled broadly. "Lawrence always means all the cruel things he says. The only time he feels head and shoulders above the crowd is when he's standing on someone else's face. But thank you for caring how I might feel. How are you?"

"Who, me?" Eric asked, picking a last piece of straw from his tunic sleeve. "I'm fine." He didn't go on to say that he was, in a sense, disappointed that Jack had arrived when he did. The line was clearly drawn now between himself and Lawrence, and it would need to be crossed sometime. This just delayed the inevitable.

Jack seemed to read his mind. "You could have handled it yourself, I know. But he is big, and I hate to watch my friends get hurt."

Eric smiled wanly. Jack Lackin considered him a friend? He didn't really know how he felt about that. Many of the squires felt Jack was the wrong kind of person to associate with. He was, after all, only a trashman, and he did, at times, seem to lack any real grasp of how to make progress up the ladder of court society. Eric recalled that he had himself at times used the nickname "Lackinsense" to describe Jack's attitudes, for with his tattered clothes and smudged face, the garbageman seemed unconcerned about what others thought of him.

And then, of course, there were the rumors.

It was widely whispered among people of the city that Jack had once been highly regarded in the High City, that ultimate ring of their home that raised its lofty spires above the clouds.

Some said he'd been a friend and confidant to the very King himself, standing at the King's right hand. But in what capacity? Everyone knew that the Archlord Michael advised the King on military matters and commanded the assembled armies. Everyone knew the Archlord Gabriel functioned as the King's chief ambassador, conveying all messages of any importance to the kingdom. What, then, had been Jack's function? The most often quoted rumor was that, before his fall, Jack Lackin had been the court jester, adding the relief of laughter to court affairs and helping all members of the High Council not to take themselves too seriously.

Unfortunately—according to the rumor—Jack Lackin had gone too far. Jesting had to be a risky business, for who could know how the King would respond to any particular joke? He knew from experience that a smart remark at the wrong moment could quickly get a person into deep trouble. What had Jack said that caused the King to expel him from the shining palace? What comment had been so rude that Jack was now assigned to the garbage heap? No one had any idea, though there was plenty of speculation. Eric was too polite to ask. Still, it seemed to make little sense to associate with an outcast. And Eric certainly didn't want the man regarding himself as Eric's protector.

"Look," he began lamely, "I appreciate your dropping by, but I really do need to get these things all polished before nightfall, so I—"

"Need any help?" Jack shrugged. "I can polish with the best of them—"

"Nooo," Eric answered, stretching the word out to make his refusal of the offer as polite as possible. "It's my job, and I'd best handle it on my own."

"And of course," Jack grinned, "my tasks just keep on piling up around me as well. There never seems to be any shortage of garbage! See you later, Eric," he waved, and Lackin stepped out of the stables. Before Eric could feel any relief at being left alone, Jack popped his head back inside and warned, "You've got another visitor coming."

Then, Jack's face disappeared, leaving Eric to grumble to himself, "Who now?"

He didn't actually groan when Winnie glided through the stable door a moment later. It wouldn't have made any difference anyway—Winnie wouldn't have heard it. Winnie was a talker, and Eric didn't even try to get in a word of welcome. He just picked the next piece of armor off the pile and found his rag, then sat down to polish while he listened. He knew it would be a while before he had any opportunity to respond.

"You have no idea what they expect of me in that kitchen!" Winnie was saying, flinging her long reddish-blonde hair over her shoulder in obvious irritation. The basket that hung on her right elbow bounced responsively. "I think if it weren't for me the whole operation would grind to a halt! First I have to scrub the cooking pans—and not just a few of them either. I mean I wash every single cooking pan in the whole kitchen, and there must be a thousand you know, a thousand cooking pans each in various stages of . . ." She went on from there. Eric looked up at her with apparent attention written on his features, but this sounded too much like polishing armor to hold his interest. His mind drifted elsewhere, to subjects more to his liking.

Like Winnie herself. Not that he would admit publicly what he thought of her—nor even, really, could he yet admit his feelings to himself—but he did know he felt better whenever Winnie was around, even if he did tend to complain about her visits.

He wouldn't have called her beautiful. Eric saved that word for the older ladies of the court who sat together in dazzling array at tournament or at table. They drew the admiring eyes of all the squires, distracting the lads from their duties, while they themselves giggled and blushed and pointed out one knight or another. *No, Winnie wasn't beautiful,* Eric thought as he shined a gilded visor. But she did look—composed. Her bright green eyes were both friendly and smart. She had an air of confidence about her that he found attractive. She seemed to be in control of herself.

Uh oh, Eric thought. She'd suddenly stopped talking and was gazing at him expectantly, those green eyes faintly accusing. "What?" he asked, and the accusation in her gaze grew firmer.

"You weren't even listening to me, were you?"

"I was listening!" he said—a bit too defensively, he realized, to be convincing.

"Then what did I say?" she asked, arching an eyebrow exactly like a schoolmistress might when giving an exam question too tough to be answered.

Eric shook his head and shrugged, "Something about cake pans," he mumbled, then he added gruffly, "I've got to get this finished," and he shined the helmet with renewed vigor.

"I asked you if you wanted to get out of this smelly stable to eat this picnic I fixed." She unhooked her basket from her elbow and waved it under his nose. He could smell the bread, freshly baked. "It's a gorgeous day out," she announced, "and you work too hard anyway. Now come on." She jerked the basket back over her arm and walked toward the door, pausing there to look back imperiously over her shoulder. At that moment Eric could think of nothing he'd rather do than be with this girl, but why did she need to be so bossy about it? Convention demanded he sigh heavily and toss aside his rag as if in resignation. He just couldn't appear too eager . . .

2

THE TRUMPET OF DOOM

He let her precede him out into the sunlight and across the packed dirt of the parade ground. Eric found it a bit embarrassing to walk beside Winnie since she was half a foot taller. Besides, it was rather nice to watch the sun glitter on her hair. It was very fine, and it took only the slightest of breezes to stir it up into a glossy halo around her shoulders. Winnie had turned willowy in the last year or so, and, as he followed her across the wide expanse of exercise yard, he was amazed again at how rapidly she had changed. She looked back over her shoulder, saw where his gaze was directed, and frowned. "What are you looking at?" she demanded.

"I don't know," Eric shrugged. But of course he did know—and she knew, and it pleased her to know he was noticing the changes in her.

The sun was high and hot in the sky. Anyone wearing armor at this hour would bake like a loaf of Winnie's wonderful bread. A low stone wall bordered one side of the parade ground, and she led him to it and plopped the basket down between them. Here they could sit and look down over the valley where they'd grown up together, or they could turn and gaze at the High City of the King, looming magnificently above them.

Though they'd both grown up in its presence, only recently had they become impressed with the High City's splendor. It stood on a mountain in the midst of a trio of mountains, its pointed spires reaching higher than the rocky crags around it. Like the mountains, it ascended like stair steps, culminating in a glistening peak of clustered towers that shined like snow. The spire could be seen at any distance from the valley below—if not obscured by the clouds. While the entire High City appeared to be carved from the same strata of white marble, each individual palisade or rampart seemed to have been designed by a different architect. All were unique, and each demanded separate appraisal by the eye. Yet for all their diversity, the buildings complemented and amplified one another. Each tower was different, but all obviously belonged.

From their vantage point below, the High City looked utterly tranquil. While they knew it was constantly bustling with business, they rarely saw any activity up there. It was far different from the chaos in the busy intersections below them in the valley. At their feet stretched what they'd always regarded as "the city"—their home. While it had always seemed vast, Eric really didn't begin to conceive of its enormity until he'd been brought up here to serve. So many people! He felt very small at the moment—insignificant, really. This was a large stable, quarters for a sizable contingent of the King's warriors. Yet he knew it was only one of many such stables that ringed the High City, passing all the way around the mountain to its far side. *What is it like on the other side of the mountain? Are stables there constructed just as this one is?* he wondered. Or would he feel them odd, and himself out of place, were he to fulfill his goal to one day circle the mountain? No matter. Whether they looked the same or different, the very thought that there were enormous places he'd never seen and where he didn't belong made Eric feel like a nobody.

"How's the bread?" Winnie asked him with forced brightness, and he realized she'd been talking to him for several minutes and he again hadn't been listening.

"Delicious," he mumbled, swallowing the bite he was chewing and pulling another soft chunk from its crusty shell. "It's still warm."

"Just out of the oven," Winnie smiled triumphantly. "One of thirty loaves I baked myself this afternoon. You can't believe how busy they had me today! I was running from table to table from the moment I got up this morning, and I couldn't get one thing done before somebody assigned me half-a-dozen other chores to do, all needing to be done immediately, naturally. Why do they always think it's only their particular job that needs doing?"

"I don't know," Eric empathized, his eyes sliding back up the hillside, climbing up the crystalline spires of the High City. He tried very hard to listen this time, but Winnie was saying the same things she said *every* day, and Eric had a hunger today to see and hear something different, something *new*. What he really wanted was to be up *there*, atop one of those towers, walking the parapet and issuing crisp orders to men under his command. Eric was tired of taking directions, and listening to Winnie made him feel no better. He wanted to *give* instructions for a change and watch them being obeyed.

"I wanted to show you something important, but you're not even listening to me!" Winnie shouted, and suddenly she was standing over him, angrily packing up the picnic she'd so carefully opened just moments before.

"What are you doing?" It was a stupid thing to ask. The answer was quite apparent.

"I'm leaving."

"But I haven't finished eating!" Eric protested to her back as she marched away.

"Oh yes you have!" Winnie didn't bother to turn her head as she passed the yawning doors of the stable on her way back to her kitchen.

"Fine!" Eric hollered, although he didn't feel fine. What he felt was both guilt and anger at once, and those two feelings certainly didn't add up to "fine." Embarrassed at this exchange of unpleasantries, he glanced around to see if anyone was watching. But the stable yard was as empty as always at this time of the afternoon. As he turned his head, the horizon caught his eyes and held them—that far, distant horizon, so clear, yet so far away. He longed to be on top of that great distant hill, to be seeing new sights and smelling new scents and feeling the breath of a different breeze on his face. He longed to be gone, to just run away, to live beyond the rule of the King in the dark green forests of the outlaws.

Eric sighed and the feeling passed. He knew who he was, and that was not a brigand or a cutthroat. He was a faithful, respectful, mannerly squire, trying his best to please his master. Eric cast one last look down to the valley and turned back to return to work. That's when the afternoon exploded.

That's how he remembered it later—it was as if a volcano suddenly erupted in the High City, blowing its languid citizens out of their naps and into the streets. The stable yard, empty just moments before, suddenly filled with agitated squires exchanging excited misinformation at the top of their lungs.

Eric stepped to the wall, looked down, and saw the shock waves of this explosion of activity rippling down to the rings below. He looked back at the crowds of wildly gesturing squires, slightly bemused by the fact that in the midst of this sudden information storm no one had bothered to tell him what was going on. Then he saw Winnie thrusting her way through the crowd, and the look on her face made him want to run. She looked enraged, and she was heading straight for him!

He felt his legs bump the wall, and he realized he'd been backing away. As he reached behind him to keep from tripping, the girl thrust her face into his and grabbed him by the collar exactly as Lawrence had earlier in the day.

"I'm sorry!" he blurted out, for it really did look like Winnie was about to punch him. She didn't seem to hear him as she leaned into his face and half-whispered, half-shouted:

"Eric! Somebody's *stolen* Gabriel's *trumpet!*" She clenched her jaw, regarding him sternly, like a mother with a misbehaving child, and waited for an admission of guilt.

"Gabriel's—trumpet?" Eric murmured, shrugging shoulders in confusion. Obviously this was terrible news, but for the moment he couldn't recall why.

"Eric!" Winnie scolded. "Don't you get it? Gabriel's trumpet! *The* trumpet! The trumpet of the King! It's the 'last trump,' you dummy!" She heaved a sigh heavy with disgust. "Honestly, Eric, why I bother with you I still can't—"

"The end of time trumpet?" Eric suddenly gasped, and Winnie smiled her humorless, I-told-you-so smile and nodded once firmly. "Oh my."

"There's more," the girl snapped, the crispness of her tone demanding that he shut his mouth and listen. She glared over both shoulders to insure that in the midst of the general hub-bub no one was paying them any mind, then leaned down to whisper in his ear, "The rumor is Wantsalot took it!" Her news delivered at last, Winnie leaned back and released Eric's collar, savoring the impact her words were having on him.

Eric felt stunned. Sir Wantsalot—Sir Wenceslas, really—was *his* knight. "My master?" he managed to mutter, and once again Winnie nodded. This time, however, she'd softened her features, preparing to comfort her humiliated friend. For it was obvious that was how Eric felt—humiliated. Shamed to the core. His knight a thief?

It wasn't that he particularly liked Wantsa—Wenceslas. He didn't even admire the man. He'd not chosen Sir Wenceslas to be his master. In fact, when he'd been appointed to serve as the man's squire, he'd almost refused, in spite of the honor of being chosen so young. Wenceslas had earned his disrespectful nickname: He *did* want a lot, of everything. No matter how many honors he received at tournament, he was always grumbling about those who'd received more. No matter how highly he'd been praised for his faithfulness to duty, he always complained about being passed over for truly responsible assignments. Even Eric had been a sore spot with him, for Wants—Wenceslas had argued noisily in Eric's presence that he deserved a more mature squire than this "lad fresh out of knee-pants!"

Eric had swallowed his pride and accepted the appointment. Wenceslas had seemed gradually to give the boy grudging appreciation for his diligence and loyalty. Eric had begun to convince himself that his master was even beginning to take him into his confidence.

But this! This was a betrayal beyond belief! "The trumpet of doom!" Eric murmured to Winnie, sitting down on the wall and rubbing his temples with both hands. "But what can he do with it?"

"What else?" Winnie shrugged, seating herself beside him and scooting close. "Who else would want it but—?" She didn't name the darkness. She didn't need to. No one in the city actually spoke the name of Lucifer if it wasn't absolutely necessary. The feeling was that if you named him, he might think you were calling him—and come.

"The Dark One," Eric said under his breath, and a chill gathered and shook him, then skittered down his back. His knight in league with the foe?

Lucifer. He was the reason for all the vigilance, the reason for King's knights and for armor, the reason the city practiced for war. There was one who had sworn to destroy it, who hated its King and who boasted of his own rebellion. Nor was he a powerless enemy, all talk and no fight. Lucifer's warriors won frequent skirmishes with the King's knights. These were not mere tournament battles, fought by the rules in the light of day. The Dark One's attacks were swift and deadly, leaving behind shattered bodies, broken lives, and grief-stricken survivors. They were brutal assaults, designed not to gain strategic advantage or control territory but simply to terrorize the citizenry. Sometimes these attacks even took place within the walls of the lower city. Lucifer wanted always to remind them that he could do it. The Dark One struck without warning whenever vigilance failed, whenever the city's protectors relaxed. Eric hated and feared him.

And what would the Dark One do if he should ever lay hands on the trumpet of doom?

The Trumpet of Doom

No one knew much about that trumpet. Most believed that a single note blown from its ancient brass tubing would bring all activity to an instant halt. The clouds would peel back from the spires of the High City, and the King would descend through the air, visible to everyone on every side of the mountain. The dead would rise to meet him, time itself would stop, and all the mountain would become part of the High City, down to the lowliest wall. Common paving stones would turn to gold, and the walls of wattle huts would turn to alabaster. There would never again be sickness or gloom or rain or misery or trouble—and all of this from a single blast upon that mighty horn!

But could the trumpet be sounded prematurely? Could any citizen summon enough breath to blow it, or was Gabriel alone qualified to blow a blast upon its mouthpiece? Some said that the trumpet simply could not be sounded until the King was ready for it to sound, no matter who might try to blow a note upon it. But what if it could? What if Sir Wantsalot himself should put the instrument to his lips and try to blow—what would happen? Could a mere *mortal* bring about the end of time?

And should the Dark One possess the trumpet—what then? Suppose Lucifer was to put that mouthpiece to his lips! Suppose he blew—he would surely have the breath to blow it, for weren't he and Gabriel and Michael all made exactly the same? Suppose the dead of the lower city rose to rally to Lucifer's black banner and not to the King's! Suppose one discordant note brought the high towers tumbling down! Suppose . . .

Other trumpets were sounding now, all around him, and squires like himself were racing to saddle their masters' horses and find their masters' mail. A half-dozen boys knelt beside Eric's pile, sorting through it in search of a missing breastplate or hauberk or helmet. Several of them glanced up at him scornfully. Dazed by it all, Eric turned back to Winnie.

"Are you certain it was *my* knight?" he whispered.

"Wenceslas was seen near the trumpet's case," she said with absolute certainty. "Then he disappeared, and the trumpet was missing also. I'm sorry, Eric," she added, sadly putting a hand on his shoulder, "but, yes, I'm afraid it was."

Eric moaned and cradled his head in his hands. "What am I going to do?"

Winnie shrugged. "Go find him, of course. Get it back." Eric jerked his head up to stare at the girl, but Winnie just met his frown with her confident smile and announced, "And I'm going with you!"

3

WHO WILL GO?

"Y̱ou?" Eric asked.

"Well of course me!" Winnie responded, hands balling into fists and plopping immediately upon her slim hips.

Uh oh, Eric thought, *I've made her angry again*. "That's not what I meant," he said lamely.

"What did you mean?" Winnie demanded.

"I didn't mean you shouldn't go—I only meant—why me? Why us? Why should we consider ourselves qualified to do this? I mean, look around." Eric gestured at the furious activity all about them. "Obviously there's been a general alarm. The King is sending out an army of searchers—" He stopped himself, suddenly remembering his earlier encounter with Lawrence. Was this the quest Sir Leffingwell had planned to embark upon in the morning—the quest to recover Gabriel's trumpet?

"Obviously," Winnie agreed. "But if everyone else is going," she asked, her green eyes wide and round in a look of mock innocence, "then why shouldn't we go, too?"

"Why?" he murmured, thinking for reasons. In fact, he had no reason why they shouldn't, other than the fact that he hadn't thought of it. It bothered him, too, that Winnie seemed so insistent upon the idea. He was learning things about Winnie today—unsettling things. "We're too young," Eric said finally.

Winnie snorted and stood up, "Well you may be," she said, "but I'm sure not."

"We're the same age!" Eric argued, his face pinched with uncertainty.

"I thought so, too," she responded disdainfully, "but evidently you think you're nothing but a child. Very well, if you'll not go with me I'm going to find someone who will." She turned her back on him.

"Wait a minute!" Eric shouted and she looked back at him coolly. "Won't you get in trouble for leaving your kitchen duties?"

"What if I do?" Winnie shrugged.

"Listen, Eric, what's happened today changes everything. Don't you see that? If the Dark One should get the trumpet, that's the end of everything as we know it! Time stops. Evil wins," she said with a suddenly reasonable tone of voice as she sat on the wall beside him. "There are times in our lives when our destinies are thrust into our own hands, to do with as we choose. It may not happen often, and once we choose a course it may be years before we get a chance to choose again which way we'll go. But for me, Eric, this day is one of those crossroad days, a day when I can choose the life I'll lead—at least for now. All I'm saying is that this could be a crossroad day for you, too."

"But—" Eric began, then stopped. He didn't have anything to say, really. It was still hard for him to grasp the fact that his life had been changed this afternoon. Eric liked order in his life.

"But what, Eric?" Winnie asked, earnestly, yet kindly. "I know you're very responsible, and this is the task you've been assigned to do." She gestured around the stable at the other boys. Warhorses were being readied by this time. Leather harnesses decorated with gold and silver and brightly painted metal were being slipped into place and buckled. Brilliant saddles with matching silk skirts were being tossed onto the broad backs of proud stallions.

Who Will Go?

"But think of this," she continued. "Your master is gone. How can you get in trouble for leaving? In fact," she went on quickly, "isn't it your duty to seek him out? Suppose," Winnie asked, warming to her argument, "that your master has been forced into stealing the trumpet by some sinister plot we know nothing about! Suppose he's out there, somewhere, needing your help!" Winnie gestured toward the mountains—those same distant, mysterious mountains that had beckoned Eric earlier.

Winnie was right. The world was suddenly different. Eric stood up and gazed off where she pointed, over the lower city toward the fields and the forest beyond. His heart pounded furiously. He felt both terrified and exhilarated. He should go. There was suddenly no question at all in his mind that he wanted to! He took a deep breath and nodded. "All right," he muttered. "I'll get my things."

"I'll go to the kitchen and start getting our provisions," Winnie whispered excitedly, and she started to bolt away. This time Eric grabbed her arm to spin her around.

"Our provisions?" he asked. "I mean—I think you're right. I've got to go. But what's your stake in all this, Winnie? You don't have to."

Winnie shook loose her arm and gazed at him fiercely. "My stake in this is that I want to go!" She growled, and Eric shrugged and backed away. He knew better than to argue with Winnie when she was this determined. "Besides," she added with a forgiving smile and a conspiratorial twinkle in her eye, "I know where he went."

"You do?" Eric blurted out, grabbing for her in surprise even as Winnie danced out of his reach. "Why didn't you say so?"

"You didn't ask!" she hissed. Then she spun around and took off toward the kitchen at a dead run.

"Winnie!" he shouted. "How far?"

She turned to look back uncertainly. "What?"

"How far are we going? How many days do we pack for? Will we be gone a week, two weeks—"

"Pack for a month!" she shouted. "But don't worry about food. I'll get that. And hurry!" he heard her shout as she disappeared around the corner. "I'll be right back!"

Left alone, Eric struggled to bring the jumble of his thoughts together. What had he just done? What had he agreed to? He glanced again at the horizon, remembering his longing to travel to that distant mountain. Suddenly he found himself committed to actually going there, to passing through those threatening woods on the way, and Eric found reality far different from the dream. His stomach seemed to flip all the way over.

What should he do now? Pack, of course. But what? What would be needed for such a journey? They couldn't walk all that way, so they needed a mount of some kind. Which horse? Sir Wenceslas had three. Which one had he taken—or had he taken any of them? Had he slipped off in the night, taking nothing with him but the trumpet?

And what about armor? They would be passing through dangerous territory. He would have to protect not only himself but Winnie as well. His master had several suits of armor, some designed more for show than for action, others more practical in design and construction. Eric found himself walking briskly toward the barracks where all sets were stored.

Suddenly he stopped. "This is ridiculous," he murmured to himself. "My master's not responsible for this! He can't be. Winnie is surely mistaken! I bet he's in his apartment right now, grumbling at how all the noise and confusion is interrupting his nap!" With that, Eric swung aside the barracks door and walked down the corridor to the quarters he shared with his master.

While a knight's living quarters were not opulent, they were certainly comfortable. Wenceslas had several apartments set aside for his personal use, which he was free to occupy or to assign to others as he chose. He also owned a villa in the lower city, not far from where Eric's parents lived. The knights furnished their quarters as they chose, and Wenceslas had spent rather lavishly—other knights would say too lavishly—to decorate this area in accordance with his tastes. That was part of

Wantsalot—Wenceslas'—reputation. He always found good reasons to spend far more than necessary. Eric knew that his master regularly spent more than he had. This had already caused problems between Wenceslas and his superiors. *Is that the reason for this theft?* Eric found himself wondering. Once again he shoved the whole preposterous idea from his mind. Sir Wenceslas, the thief of Gabriel's trumpet? Ridiculous!

Moments later, Eric's certainty of his master's loyalty stood severely shaken. Sir Wenceslas's was indeed gone. Eric knew which treasures Wenceslas prized above all others. These were missing, as was the knight's favorite armor, a suit of mail constructed to be both comfortable and protective.

Eric's sense of disappointment and betrayal deepened. How could his master do such a thing! How could he show such complete disdain for the vows he'd taken the morning he'd been dubbed a knight? How could anyone turn his back on such a commitment?

"Need some help?" someone said behind him, and Eric whirled around, horribly startled. Jack Lackin, the garbageman, smiled and shrugged.

"Why did you sneak up on me like that?" Eric scolded.

"I didn't intend to surprise you. I just thought you might need some help."

"For what?" Eric snapped, suddenly very protective of both his master's reputation and his own secret plans.

"To get ready," Jack said simply. "You are going after him, aren't you?"

"After who?" Eric asked, but he could feel his face flushing as he spoke. He'd never been a good liar.

Jack didn't smile. "After your master. It appears that he took something that didn't belong to him."

"How do you know that?" Eric demanded, his voice far harsher than it needed to be. He was sorry about that, for he knew that Jack Lackin wasn't to blame. Still, the man made an easy target for anger which couldn't be directed anywhere else.

Strangely, Jack didn't seem to mind. He just shrugged and answered, "Oh, I just added up all the things I know, and that seemed the most reasonable explanation. Your master is missing, is he not? And he did take with him certain things he's told you he couldn't live without?"

Eric debated briefly whether to try to defend Wenceslas any further. Then he plopped down on his master's bed. "Why would he do such a thing?" Eric asked aloud, not of Jack, but of this room which bore mute but elegant testimony to the life his master had apparently ruined.

Jack sat on the bed beside him and sighed heavily before answering. "Why does anyone do anything?"

"What do you mean?" Eric grumbled.

"Just that," Lackin shrugged. "Why do people—apparently bright, articulate, one might even guess wise people—do things that spoil the lives they've labored so carefully to construct?"

"Why did you?" Eric blurted out before giving any thought at all to what he was saying. Behind his words was that old rumor, that tale repeated whenever Jack passed by, that Jack Lackin had once been the jester to the King. In some versions of the story, he had actually used the title "Lackinsense," although others believed that nickname came later—after his fall.

As court jester Jack had been entitled to full access to all the King's affairs, for the purpose of any jester was to insure that the ruler never became inflated with self-importance, and how could a jester comment on things he knew nothing about? Thus, meetings between the King and the High Staff—meetings involving Michael and Gabriel and the others—had all had as an uninvited observer Jack Lackin. Of course, in those days there had also been another participant: Lucifer had shared in the decisions of state, debating and challenging while plotting his rebellion—and somehow Jack Lackinsense had known.

According to the story, the jester had begun to mock the entire council for its blindness—some said to try to open their eyes, but most believed just because Lackin could see what others couldn't and was proving himself superior. Sharper and sharper his jabs grew, until at last he was needling even the King, and without subtlety at all. Lucifer, too, he mocked. Some believed it was Lackin's barbs which goaded the Dark Prince into action. Rebellion broke out in the High City, a rebellion that scarred the entire land. Battles waged in uppermost spires had effects which rippled downward through the lower rings. It soon became apparent that Lucifer had drawn much of the common citizenry into his conspiracy.

The plan, of course, had failed. The conspirators had been routed and had fled from the city on horseback or on foot, streaming outward through every gate to hide as outlaws in the woods beyond. Soon thereafter there had been changes made in the High City. Among the changes was the expulsion of Lackinsense.

His jokes had been remembered, so the story went. He had obviously had prior knowledge of the rebellion and had made light of the truth instead of reporting it. If he couldn't tell the difference between the gemstones of truth and the garbage of conspiracy, let him spend his days sorting through the refuse of the lower city. Jack the jester had been condemned to serve as Lackinsense the garbageman. At least, that's how the tale was told.

"Why did I what?" Jack asked Eric directly. There was neither guile nor bile in his voice. It was just a straightforward question, and Eric found it impossible to answer.

"I—I've just—I don't—."

"Never mind," Jack shrugged, and he turned to survey the wall where the knight's armor hung on display. "Now what should you take?"

Eric had an odd feeling, one he couldn't explain but fully understood. Without his asking, Jack had forgiven him—completely and immediately—for his insulting suspicion. It was such an instant, gracious forgiveness that Eric couldn't help but feel drawn to this man. But it also made him wonder. *What is*

Jack's real story? What actually happened in those crystalline hallways high above?

"You'll need a sword, of course," Lackin continued, and he reached up to pull one down off the wall. "Is this too heavy?" He passed it to Eric, who had to take it in both hands.

"Ah—maybe," Eric murmured.

Jack pursed his lips and looked back at the wall. "It seems to be the lightest one here."

"It is," Eric nodded.

"I guess you realize the rest of this is a little large, too."

It was indeed. Wenceslas was a big man, and Eric was only half-grown. He could wear it, but he would look like a turtle drawn into its shell—hardly the dashing figure of a knight he'd often imagined himself cutting.

"You could go without it, I guess," Jack shrugged doubtfully.

"I'd be cut to pieces in my first encounter," Eric grumbled. "I'll have to pad it, of course, or my whole back will be blistered by nightfall, but I'd better wear it. Winnie will be depending on me."

"Right," Jack Lackin agreed, and he began quickly pulling down the best pieces to assemble the most workable set.

Eric smiled "You do that so well. Did you spend time as a squire yourself?"

"I know quite a bit about armor," Jack said cryptically, but he gave no further explanation. He just worked on quickly until Eric was fully encased in a suit of armor which would give him maximum protection. "Now you need a horse," Jack announced, and Eric nodded in agreement, although that wasn't easy to do. He bumped his chin against the too-big breastplate. "This way," Lackin instructed, and Eric followed him back out of the barracks toward the stables.

Eric appreciated Jack's initiative. He would have found it almost impossible to walk boldly into the stables alone and to take one of Wenceslas's horses by himself. He was sure he would have felt the accusing eyes of all the other squires, arrayed as he was in his master's colors. With Jack leading, however, he found it easy—and really, no other squire had time to bother with him at the moment. They were all too busy getting their own masters prepared to ride.

As Eric had guessed, Endeavor was gone. The black stallion was Wenceslas's fastest horse and would be the most difficult to see in the dark. Since the knight had evidently slipped away sometime in the pre-dawn hours, that choice made the most sense. It meant that Eric was left to pick between Glory or George. There really was no choice to be made: Glory was a show horse, a beautiful roan mare that Wenceslas rode only in parades and to social gatherings. George was his only warhorse, a huge chestnut gelding with the bland disposition of a peasant. Much as he'd like to ride Glory, when outfitted in full armor he would have to take George. George could carry anything.

"You'll need the mare for your lady, of course," Lackin murmured, and Eric wheeled around to stare at him in shock.

"My lady?" he gasped.

Jack Lackin shrugged and smiled. "She thinks she's your lady, whether you do or not."

"You mean Winnie?"

"She's going with you, isn't she?"

Eric scowled. "How do you know so much about all this?"

Jack Lackin smiled broadly, showing his pearly teeth. "Haven't you heard? Garbagemen know everything!" He turned and started saddling Glory, continuing over his shoulder, "Whether she's your lady or not, she'll need a horse to ride, and she certainly won't find one in the kitchen. Since she's not too heavy, this one can carry most of your provisions as well."

Eric said nothing. His privacy was very important to him. Did everyone know his business?

Jack seemed almost to read his mind. "It isn't easy," he said quietly, "to find yourself the topic of everyone's conversation. You've done nothing yourself, Eric, and yet by association with your master, some will now think you capable of anything." Lackin neatly completed outfitting Glory and turned to help Eric lift George's saddle over the great beast's back. "I've had a bit of experience with notoriety myself, you know," he smiled sadly, passing the strap beneath George's belly for Eric to slip through the buckle, then cinching it tight. "I can think of only one advantage to it."

Eric was surprised. There was an advantage to having a bad reputation? "What?" he asked grimly.

"You learn to examine the influence of your actions on others," Jack answered. "You find that what you do really does make a difference to the lives of those around you." Jack stepped around George and walked to the door to the stable where the afternoon sun poured its rays into the somber darkness. He waved Eric toward him, saying, "I have something for you." Eric shuffled hesitantly toward him as Jack pulled an object from a very deep pocket and held it up to the light.

"It's—a bell," said Eric, his voice full of puzzle.

"It is indeed," Jack Lackin murmured, and he tossed the acorn-sized bell into the air and caught it. Its jingle was unmistakable. "A jester's jinglebell," he said, taking Eric's hand and placing the bell in it. "It's from my cap."

Eric blinked twice, finally stammering, "Th-then th-the stories about—about you being in the High City are—are true?"

Jack Lackin's face took on a faraway look, and his head inclined backward as if to gaze up through the stable walls at the High City itself. "True?" He shrugged. "True as the stories they'll soon be whispering about Eric the squire." He turned back to look George in the face and pat the big horse's shoulders. "Are you ready to travel, my friend?" George made no comment. He just eyed Jack stolidly and waited. "Carry the bell with you, Eric," said Jack, still gazing into George's eyes. "Let it remind you that not everything people say is true—and that you have a friend who believes in you. Come on, George," he finished, slipping the horse's bridle into place, then leading him around to the stable door and out.

Eric held the bell before him, turning it in the light and regarding it with some degree of awe. It symbolized something, obviously, to Jack, but Eric had the feeling it meant far more than he as yet could understand. He would have to store this bell in a safe place and think more about it when he had time. He heard Winnie's voice outside the stable, calling to him.

It was time to go.

4

On the Road

As they rode down one of the many cobbled streets that descended through the city, Eric watched himself as if some other person sat inside this suit of armor. They were on the road, and it was all too incredible to believe. He could feel the heat building up inside this metal suit. He was well aware of the clanking the too-large helmet made against the too-large breastplate—yet he still had difficulty convincing himself that it was actually he who led this little parade down the mountain toward the gate. He kept expecting some true knight to appear out of nowhere to order him to get down off of George and go back to the barracks where he belonged.

No knight appeared. The people in the city had their own concerns this day, and for all the frantic activity around them, very few glances were thrown at them.

What attention they did receive appeared to be directed at Jack Lackin. It was Jack who had boosted Eric into this saddle. It was Jack who had led both George and Glory out of the stable and ignored Winnie's excited babbling long enough to get her mounted on Glory's back and to get their provisions for the trip stored in large sacks behind her. It was Jack who now followed them down the street, smiling and waving at those who recognized him. Everyone seemed to know the garbageman.

Eric appreciated Jack's help. He really didn't know how he could have gotten himself into this saddle without it and was equally concerned with how he was to get down. Still, it was a bit embarrassing to have a garbageman along as a squire, and he was beginning to wonder how far Jack intended to travel with them.

Winnie seemed oblivious to Jack's company, thrilled as she was with her mount and with the whole idea of this adventure. "Look at us! Look at us, Eric!" she whispered loudly from behind him. "We're actually going! Can you believe it? You and I are actually on the road!"

"I know that, Winnie," he answered soberly, feeling the need to counterbalance her enthusiasm with a realistic look at their situation. "A squire, a kitchen maid, and a trashman embarking on a quest to save the kingdom. And I don't even know where we're going—"

He heard Winnie's exasperated sigh, "I don't know why you can't just enjoy this for a few minutes! It's what you wanted to do with your life! I'd think you'd be thrilled!"

"Perhaps I would be thrilled if I felt there was any sense to all of this," he replied. He kept his eyes fixed straight ahead—he couldn't twist his head comfortably anyway. "I mean, here we are leaving in the late afternoon! Trips are supposed to be begun in the morning! How far do you expect us to get before we have to stop and camp?"

"A ways," Winnie answered firmly. "And we'll be ahead of the others. It looks to me like everyone is making preparations to leave tomorrow morning. This way, when we rise we'll already be well on our way."

"To where, Winnie?" he called back over his shoulder. "You still haven't told me where we're going."

"In good time, Sir Knight," Winnie teased, but her words made every muscle in Eric's neck tighten. He was not a knight—not yet—and that was too exalted a title for anyone to throw around in jest. He held his tongue, though. No point in antagonizing his travel partner this early in the journey. He had enough to contend with already. They would soon pass within a few hundred feet of his home, and he was afraid one of his relatives would recognize him. What would his parents say about all this? He told himself that he really didn't care about his father's opinion. His father was a man who'd never had any ambition to rise above where he was, and frankly, Eric considered him an embarrassment. His mother, though, had poured her whole life into helping him achieve his dream. What if his actions today ruined his future? How would he ever explain it to her?

He tried to glance to the left and right without turning his head. He felt terribly self-conscious in the armor of Sir Wenceslas. People in this area of the city knew this armor. *Why hadn't they chosen a different road down through the city?* he thought to himself angrily.

He heard a sudden shout from his left. "It's Wantsalot!" A crowd suddenly clustered around to stare up at them. He urged George to move faster. George, of course, took a dim view of that, carrying as he was the huge weight of his true master's armor as well as his master's squire, along with those supplies Jack didn't feel Glory could carry. The old warhorse even seemed to slow down.

"Where's the trumpet?" somebody shouted.

"Get in front of him!" "Block his path!" "Stop him!" other voices cried, and soon it was impossible for George to make any headway at all. The cobbled corridor was clogged with people.

A hand grabbed Eric's knee and nearly unhorsed him, but he managed to hold himself in the saddle and tried again to spur his mount forward.

"Eric?" Winnie said doubtfully behind him.

"It's all right, Winnie, we just need to get—through—these—"

But there was no getting through the crowd. A tall, broad-faced man had seized George's bridle, and the horse obligingly

On the Road

stopped. Glory did not follow suit. She kicked her way sideways and pranced forward until Winnie sat even with Eric.

"You're not Wantsalot," the man snarled, and Eric recognized him. He was a local fish seller who considered himself one of the leaders of the neighborhood. Eric pretended not to know him as the man shouted, "What are you doing, boy?"

"Let go of my bridle, sir," Eric shouted, trying to force authority into his voice. That was a mistake—how high-pitched it sounded!

"Who are you?" the man demanded, shoving his face up over the edge of Eric's saddle. "Why are you wearing a knight's armor and riding a knight's horse?"

"I'm squire to Sir Wenceslas, riding in quest of my master!" Eric shouted, trying his best to jerk George's reins free from the man's grip.

"Wait! I recognize you! You grew up just two streets over! You're just a boy!" the man snarled. "Get down off that horse and get out of that stolen armor!"

"I'd not noticed your armor, sir," said Jack Lackin genially as he pushed himself between Eric's stirrup and this man who'd blocked the road. "Are you a man who has chosen to do the King's bidding? Or are you rather—" Jack sniffed the man's tunic dramatically "—a fish merchant?"

"You know very well who I am, Jack Lackinsense, as I very well know you! You have no part in this affair, so—"

"On the contrary, Gene Willoughby, I have much to do with this affair. The lad and his lady are friends of mine who have undertaken to right a wrong. They may be young, but they're also able and eager. If this is a lad about men's work, could it be because 'men' such as yourself are not eager enough to do it?" As he spoke Jack moved ever closer to the burly fish merchant, and Gene Willoughby retreated with every step. Now, in one motion, Jack flipped the man's hand off of George's bridle and pivoted backward to slap the animal on the rump. George responded with a surprised leap forward that quickly parted the crowd, and Glory followed eagerly in his wake. Once free of the

Gabriel's Trumpet

press and moving downwards, George apparently found it harder to stop than to keep on clopping. Glory matched his pace joyfully. Eric and Winnie were soon riding through almost deserted streets. When George seemed prepared to slow down again, Eric recalled the spurs attached to the heels of this armor—and used them.

Now it was a question of whether Eric could stay in the saddle at all, for George suddenly hurtled forward, clattering down the incline with a thunderous noise. He was, after all, a warhorse, and those spurs meant only one thing: a full-speed charge into battle. Eric dragged backwards on the reins but didn't regain control of his steed until they reached the gate in the bottom-most city wall. Even then George didn't stop completely. He just slowed to a businesslike canter and passed under the portcullis and onto the drawbridge. Eric had time only to wave at the startled guards before he and Winnie were . . .

Free. Free! Out of the city and into the fields and free at last! And suddenly all the anxiety and worry Eric had been feeling throughout the whole afternoon disappeared. For the first time all day he felt the genuine thrill Winnie had been urging upon him, for—knighted or not—he was an armor-clad warrior riding off on a quest of true importance to his Lord and King! This was, indeed, why he'd been born!

Winnie quickly caught up with him, looking breathless and frightened. She reined in Glory and peered over at him. "Are you all right?" she shouted.

"Never better!" Eric shouted back, then said, "We've not much time before nightfall. Let's let these animals run!" Once again he spurred George's flanks, and that four-legged soldier sprang forward with Glory hard on his heels. They galloped past the vast grape orchards that ringed this side of the city, ignoring the purple harvest that hung heavy from the vines. They rode through crossroads without stopping, across wooden bridges that noisily announced their sudden arrival, then just as swiftly fell silent behind them, past high hedgerows that hid whatever took place beyond them from any rider's eye. They rode toward the forest that had seemed so near from high on the city walls above. Now it seemed far away.

It was George who decided they should stop. As if it suddenly registered with the great beast that they'd been charging for some time and hadn't yet met an enemy, he shortened his stride, snorted, then stopped. Glory, carrying far less weight, danced on beyond him, and Winnie had to wheel around and come back. As she met Eric's gaze her eyes glowed with excitement—just as he supposed his own eyes must be. Neither of them said anything at first. They just looked at one another, then burst out laughing.

"Are you having fun?" Winnie asked, delighted that she knew in advance his answer.

"I've never had so much fun in my entire life!" Eric shouted back, and Winnie beamed. She was the kind of person who could never thoroughly enjoy any experience unless everyone around her was enjoying it as much. Given Eric's stoic personality, this simply couldn't happen often when she was with him. To see him so genuinely enthralled by something that had been her idea thrilled her. She sat back in Glory's saddle and smiled at him almost smugly. "How far shall we go before we camp?" she asked.

"I don't know," Eric shrugged. "Where are we going?"

A doubtful expression flickered across her face, but she hid it quickly and turned Glory around to face the forest. "There," she said firmly.

A bit too firmly? Eric wondered. "Where, exactly?"

"The forest," she called out, not looking back, and she urged Glory forward. That horse was happy to respond, but George was obviously not. He moved only grudgingly, which irritated Eric, for just at the moment he really wanted a good look at Winnie's face—

"Where in the forest, exactly?" he asked, a hint of the old anxiety edging back into his voice.

"How should I know, exactly?" Winnie replied with a shrug. "I've never been there before." She still wasn't looking back at him, which only caused Eric's concern to grow.

"But you do know where we're going generally?" he pleaded with her back.

"Of course!" But Winnie obviously didn't care for this line of questioning. She pushed Glory into a trot to put some distance between them. George plodded after, his pace not varying one bit. Eric had to content himself with following Winnie's lead . . .

5

EMERALD GREEN

Maybe Winnie was right, Eric thought as he took a deep breath and tried to enjoy again the scenery that surrounded them. Maybe he did worry too much.

If he had his wish he would play all the time and allow others to worry for him. But from an early age, Eric had felt responsible for everything and everybody. It seemed the weight of knighthood had been bred into him, and he could not escape its demands or its burdens.

When the subject came up, Winnie always said she didn't want him to—she just wished he could enjoy it all more. He sighed again, deeply. He would try. "Slow down, will you?" he called to her, but she pretended not to hear. Then he remembered when she'd gotten mad at him that morning, and why.

"What was it you were trying to show me this morning?" he shouted hopefully, and while Winnie didn't turn around, she did seem to rein Glory in a bit. Plodding, George closed the gap between them, and after a moment, Eric was riding right behind her.

"I thought you weren't interested in that," Winnie sniffed. Eric hadn't really been certain she was pouting until just now.

"It's not that I wasn't interested. I was just—busy." She didn't reply. Evidently she was going to need more prodding to warm back up to him. "I'm sorry, Winnie. It's been a strange day. What was it you were trying to show me? You sounded excited."

He was riding even with her now, and could look across to see her chewing her lip contemplatively. Suddenly she announced, "I'll show it to you this evening, after we've camped."

"You brought it with you?" he asked.

"Why not? It isn't that heavy!"

"Fine," Eric nodded, and he turned his eyes back to the road. He had no interest in arguing—he just wanted company as he traveled into this unknown land. While Eric and his family had taken occasional trips outside the walls, he couldn't ever remember having passed this way before.

The forest continued to recede before them. What from the city's heights looked like a sharp divide between plowed fields and the treeline turned out to be a much more gradual change. It wasn't long before they realized they wouldn't make the forest proper before nightfall. They passed now through parklands—fields and meadows interrupted by clumps of trees. It was beautiful, pleasant countryside, and Winnie and Eric slowed their pace without knowing it as they fell into a relaxed conversation about nothing in particular. As daylight faded they began looking for possible camping sites and quickly agreed on a spot between two oaks beside a stream. "You'll have to help me down," Eric said as Winnie slipped lightly from Glory's back and tied the reins to a bush.

"I knew that," the girl murmured, and she walked over to hold one of George's stirrups and offer her shoulder for Eric to lean on. He didn't dismount, really. He rather fell out of the saddle, and hit the ground beside her with a heavy clank. "Maybe we should have waited for Jack Lackin," Winnie observed with a dry smile. "He seemed to want to come with us."

"I think he just wanted to help us get on our way. Help me with these, will you?" he asked, lifting a gauntlet before her face. Winnie obligingly helped him pull it off, and working together they quickly had the armor off of Eric and strewn in a pile around him. "Whew! Hot in there. I think I'll go—" he pointed to the stream.

"Help yourself," Winnie gestured. As he went to wash in the cool water, she set up camp as if she'd been doing it for years. Eric gathered firewood, and by the time the purple sky turned black, they had both eaten their fill of the food she'd brought and were resting comfortably on blankets beside the fire.

"Now," Winnie said, just about the time Eric felt ready to turn over and go to sleep. "I want to show you what I brought." She dug around in the sack stuffed full of her belongings and pulled a bundle from it with the reverence reserved only for treasures. "Here it is," she murmured, her voice quiet but charged with excitement. Eric leaned forward, suddenly very curious, and saw fabric. Green fabric.

"It's—pretty," he said.

"Isn't it gorgeous?" Winnie gushed. "It's brocade silk, emerald green! Look at the pattern! Isn't it the most beautiful stuff you've ever seen?"

"Ahh—Unh-hunh," Eric nodded, repeating, "It's pretty," once again because he really didn't have much else to say about it. Fabric was fabric. "What's it for?"

Winnie's head cocked back in that familiar how-can-you-be-so-stupid position as she said, "What's it for? What do you *think* it's for?"

"A—dress?" Eric shrugged.

"A gown, Eric!"

"That's what I meant, a gown," Eric mumbled quickly, as Winnie continued:

"A beautiful gown, a lady's gown!" Winnie abruptly leaned forward to peer across the campfire at him, and its flames lit up her scowling expression quite vividly. "I've seen how you look at the ladies of the court, Eric, and don't tell me you don't."

"Ah—well." He wondered if the fire illuminated his blush as clearly as it did her frown.

"You don't look at me that way."

"Yes, well, they're—they're bigger. Older. You know."

"Nobody looks at me that way," Winnie murmured, her voice growing distant, and Eric realized with some relief that this wasn't pointed at him any longer but at the world in general. "They just see me as little Winnie, the baker's girl."

"Maybe now," Eric shrugged, "but as you get older I'm sure that—"

"What do you know? You spend your time practicing battle and rushing around aiding your knight and pretending to be important."

"Pretending?"

"Here we are on a truly important quest—which was my idea, remember!—and all you really have in your mind is what *you* will do, and where *you* will go, and what *you* will achieve, and how people in the city will talk about you when *you* return in victory with Gabriel's trumpet! But what about *me*, Eric? Where will I be when you're receiving the accolades of your triumph?" She held the brocade cloth under her chin and looked at it fondly. "I'll be wearing my victory dress. Emerald green."

Eric had no idea how to respond. None of what Winnie had said had been in his mind—well, maybe he'd thought about his triumphant return a little, especially during the quiet patches in their afternoon ride—but he really hadn't planned it all out in his mind. To be truthful, Eric had spent far more time imagining how he would explain his failure to recover the lost trumpet. Winnie apparently had all of it already planned out, and she obviously had far more confidence in his ability than he did himself. Could it be so? Could he actually dream of riding back up into the city a hero?

She was looking at him again—sadly, somehow. He suddenly realized why. She was right, after all—Eric spent most of his time thinking only of himself. He gazed down at the silk brocade, which seemed to glisten in the flickering light of their campfire, then raised his eyes to meet hers with a smile. "You'll look stunning in it," he announced, and he reached down to grab the edge of his blanket and pulled it tightly around him.

"Really?" she said brightly. "Do you really think so?"

"Of course. It matches your eyes." Actually, Eric couldn't tell if this was so or not. It was dark, after all, and firelight can only reveal so much. But it sounded like the things he knew the older squires said to girls when they wanted to sit with them at the table. He was glad there wasn't anyone else around to hear him saying it and to tease him about it later. Evidently, it was just the right thing to say, for Winnie responded:

"Eric! You noticed!"

"We'd better get some sleep," he said, rolling onto his back, and he liked the way his voice sounded as he said it—very masculine and protective.

"All right," he heard her say from the other side of the fire—not with much conviction, certainly, but without any challenge. He heard her rustling around for several minutes thereafter, then she grew quiet. As he waited for sleep to come, the thoughts and cares of the day began to seep back into his mind. He didn't welcome them, but they came anyway.

"Winnie?" he said.

"Yes?"

"When are you going to tell me where we're going?"

The long pause following his question did not set his mind at ease at all, but at least she did finally answer. "In the morning, Eric. I'll tell you in the morning."

"Good," he murmured. If he worried any longer after that, he didn't remember it.

6

THE RESCUE OF LEFFINGWELL

Eric woke with a start. The sun was already well up in the horizon. He jerked up to a sitting position and looked around. How had he managed to sleep so long? And on the ground, too! He must have been exhausted the night before. "Winnie?" he called.

"Right here." She was behind him about ten feet away, sitting on a rock and drinking something. Her face looked reflective, and—yes, beautiful.

"It must be mid-morning already," he muttered, rubbing sleep from his eyes. "Why didn't you wake me up?"

"I was thinking."

"About what?" he asked absently, stretching. His body was telling him that while he had indeed slept long on this cold ground, he had not necessarily slept well.

"About how to tell you I lied."

Eric suddenly was standing on his blanket, fully awake. "About what?" he asked—but he knew.

"About knowing where your master went." She looked up at him, meeting his eyes, evenly. "I don't, you know."

Eric exhaled slowly. "I didn't know that, no."

"Yes you did," she said, standing up and emptying her cup on the grass.

"I did not!" he shouted, his worries from the day before suddenly maturing into anger. "I never would have come on this quest if I'd known that!"

"Yes you would," Winnie muttered.

"I would not! Winnie, what are we doing out here? I only came because you told me you knew where Wenceslas was bound! I never would have agreed to come if I'd thought you were—"

"You wanted to come just as much as I did!" Winnie yelled back at him, equally angry. "You just needed an excuse! Well, I gave you one. I gave us both one! Think about it, Eric. How would I know where your knight was going? Do you think he would have announced it to a scullery maid? You wanted to believe I knew because more than anything you want to be a knight, to set out on adventures and accomplish something important! So I let you believe. Blame me if you want to. But don't tell me you don't want to be here, doing what we're doing. I know you better than that, Eric—probably better than you know yourself."

Eric had stopped listening and was surveying the things that needed to be picked up and packed away on the horses. "We've got to go back."

"Go back! Why?"

"Because we're just kids, Winnie. Help me pack this stuff up."

"I'm not going back!"

"Yes you are."

"I am not, and neither are you! Even Jack Lackin thought we should go. Else why would he have helped us get ready and get away?"

Eric knelt beside his blanket and began rolling it up. "You're talking about a garbageman, Winnie. I'm sure Jack Lackin would help anyone do anything they—"

The sound was unmistakable to anyone who'd spent his last two years learning war. A sword crashed against a shield somewhere not far from them—more than one sword, several at once.

"Eric?" Winnie said, her face paling. He held up his hand to still her, then listened. There came another, equally unmistakable sound. An armor-clad knight had been knocked from his horse and had crashed to the ground. Now they could hear the shouting and more noises of metal clanging against metal. There was no time to do anything but grab his sword and throw himself up onto George's back.

The warhorse was without saddle but wore his bridle still, and apparently he heard the battle sounds as well. Wheeling toward the noise he charged off through the brush, and Eric had to lay low on George's neck and clasp him tightly with arms and legs to keep from being thrown. He heard Winnie shout, "Eric! No!" from behind him, then he could hear no more—he hoped she'd have the good sense to leave their stuff scattered around the campfire, grab Glory and ride like the wind back to the city.

What they'd heard was no practice duel at arms. A King's knight had been ambushed and knocked from his horse, and was now hand-to-hand with more than one attacker. In this region he needed only one guess as to who those attackers might be: Lucifer's minions. He heard cries for aid.

"I'm coming!" he shouted at the top of his lungs and clung to George's back all the harder.

George was a big horse, a heavy horse. He made a lot of noise as he galloped toward the melee. Besides George's hoof-beats, Eric heard now behind him the quicker pounding of Glory, coming up fast behind him. Winnie had indeed grabbed Glory, but she hadn't turned for home.

Her decision may well have saved the beleaguered knight's life, for the outlaws heard them as several riders approaching rather than two, and how could they know it wasn't a band of fully armored knights? They broke off their attack and fled before Eric and Winnie could arrive on the scene—much to Eric's relief. They left behind them a badly battered knight who

The Rescue of Leffingwell

sat in the dust, blood coating his armor in two places. Eric recognized the man's helmet immediately. He'd held it in his hands just the day before.

"Sir Leffingwell!" he said as he dropped from George's back and rushed to the wounded man's side.

"Get it—off—" The man was struggling to remove that very helmet, and Eric expertly released it, drew it off, and tossed it aside.

"Are you all right?" he asked, feeling stupid even as he did.

"I'm wounded, lad," the knight snarled, "I would think you could see that for yourself." Then he exploded in rage. "Why did you run off when those brigands appeared? I told you we'd be certain to run across—" Sir Leffingwell stopped, his eyes focusing on Eric's face. "Why—you're not Lawrence."

"No, sir," Eric responded courteously, but his thoughts were anything but courteous, and they were all aimed at Lawrence. So the barrack's oldest squire had run off when attacked, had he? Eric was hardly surprised.

Winnie had arrived and now knelt beside him. "He's got a wound in the shoulder and a worse cut in the leg. Help me get him out of this." They worked quickly to free him from the dented metal plates.

"You took a lot of blows," Eric mumbled as the knight began to breathe more comfortably.

"There were three of them. Three or four. My boy ran off. You're Wantsalot's boy, aren't you?" Eric nodded, embarrassed. "Where is that fool? He's the reason I'm out here getting myself hammered on!"

"I don't know, sir," Eric replied honestly, then looked at Winnie. "Can you help me get him onto George and back to the stream? I can't even tell how badly he's injured." Before he got the words out Winnie was bringing George around and helping him pull the knight to his feet. This was no easy task, for Sir Leffingwell was a big man who obviously spent long hours at the dinner table.

"If you—unh!—don't know—unh!" Sir Leffingwell grunted as he struggled up, "what are you—ow!—what are you doing out here?"

"Same thing as you, sir," Eric replied. "I'm looking for him." How were they to get the man onto George? They couldn't hoist him onto the horse's back—they would have to lay him across it. It was the only way. "I'm sorry about this, sir, but we need to boost you up across—"

"Don't apologize, lad," the knight gasped. "You saved my life." The heavy knight chuckled and patted his large belly, exposed now that Eric had freed him of his breastplate. "It's me who should apologize, for this. Too many biscuits," he winked conspiratorially—then his face paled and he sagged against George.

"He's fainting," Winnie whispered, reaching forward with Eric to grab him again. They looked at one another, silently counted to three, then both lifted and pushed with all their might. The knight flopped across George's back, and as Eric held him in place, Winnie rushed around to grab his arms and pull him over farther. He roused himself enough to murmur, "Don't leave my armor," then passed out. Winnie rushed to collect the discarded pieces and to grab Glory's reins, and a few minutes later they were helping the knight drop back down from George's back to sprawl beside their campfire.

Winnie raced off to fill the helmet with water from the stream as Eric wrestled to get the rest of Leffingwell's armor off. The leg wound was deep, much deeper than Eric had guessed. He needed to stop the bleeding. Without really thinking of what he was doing he grabbed for Winnie's bag and began to jerk the brocade material out of it.

"No!" the girl screamed behind him. He froze as she slammed the helmet down, rushed to his side and furiously snatched her bag away.

"The man is dying."

"Then use your blanket!" she shrilled, grabbing his bedroll up off the ground and throwing it at him. He didn't know why he hadn't thought of that in the first place. As Winnie stomped away to fetch another helmet-full of water, he cut the blanket into strips with his sword and began tying a tourniquet high on the man's thigh. By the time it was in place Winnie was back with the water, and together they bathed the wound and wrapped it in the remaining strips. By the time they could turn their attention to the cut in his shoulder, Sir Leffingwell had started to shiver. They wrapped him in Winnie's blanket and rekindled the fire to keep him warm, then Eric watched without comment as Winnie folded the yards of green cloth once more and packed them carefully away at the bottom of her sack.

He didn't need to be told that she wasn't speaking to him.

7

Riding Blind

They took turns watching him throughout the day, saying very little to one another. Most of what they did say centered around the knight's care. Eric ate whenever she handed him food and watched as she paced the edge of their campsite. Her expression never changed—it was cloudy with hurt.

While he knew why she was angry, Eric didn't understand why she was angry. After all, how could a bolt of fabric be more important than the life of a King's knight?

He sighed, leaned back against the trunk of one of the oaks, and thrust his hands in his pockets. His fingers fumbled across something curious, and he pulled it out to look—then he remembered. It was the bell Jack had given him, the jinglebell from Jack's fool's cap.

This is appropriate, Eric thought grimly. Here he was, a mere squire, out in the middle of the wilderness with an angry girl and an unconscious knight, open to attack at any time. He certainly felt like a fool. As the sun slipped down toward late afternoon, Winnie wordlessly assumed watch over Sir Leffingwell. Eric rolled over to look back in the direction of the city and thought about home. *Was this homesickness?* he wondered.

He rolled onto his back and played catch with the bell until his thoughts grew fuzzy. *Good, Eric,* he scolded himself silently as he tried to fight off sleep. *Doze on off, fool, and let Lucifer cut your throat!* But despite his struggle to stay alert, he couldn't rouse himself.

When he woke with a start it was night—and Jack Lackin was sitting beside him.

"Jack!" Eric said, feeling both pleased and embarrassed—pleased to see this friend from the city; embarrassed that he and Winnie had left Jack behind. Jack's eyes seemed to read clearly his mixed feelings. "How did you find us?"

"It wasn't hard," Jack smiled. "You headed straight out the gate and away from the city and never turned to the right or the left. I just did the same."

Eric blinked a couple of times, then shook his head to clear it. This sounded a bit too incredible. He realized he was still holding Jack's bell in his right hand—and wondered aloud. "On foot?"

Jack ignored the question. Instead, he nodded toward the fire and said, "Sir Leffingwell woke up while you were napping."

"Is he going to live?" Eric asked, sitting up.

"Am I going to live?" Sir Leffingwell's jolly voice boomed out in the darkness. "Why, lad, I'm ready to ride!"

"Ready to ride?" Eric asked. Impossible! He'd dressed the wounds in this man's body just this morning—and they were deep. "How did you heal so quickly?"

"Takes more than a few cutthroats with swords to bring this old warrior down. Get a good night's sleep, lad. We'll chase the brigands down in the morning."

"I wouldn't want to push too hard too quickly, Sir Knight," Jack cautioned, rising to walk back toward the fireside where Leffingwell still rested.

"Ah, but that's the difference between us, Jack Lackin—the reason I'm a knight and you're a trashman. You never push, and I always do." Leffingwell said this in a genial tone of voice, but Eric still felt offended for Jack. He also felt somehow as if the ground had shifted beneath him. When he'd dropped off to sleep he'd been alone in the wilderness with a girl and a dying knight—but he'd also been in charge. Suddenly he felt like nothing but a squire again.

"No," Jack Lackin chuckled, clearly not bothered by Leffingwell's comment, "the real difference between us is that while I tend to act the fool, you tend to be one."

Sir Leffingwell did take offense. "You listen here!" he snarled, and he tried to reach out to grab Jack by the tunic. Instead he had to grunt in pain and grab his wounded shoulder with his other hand.

Jack raised his eyes and appeared to study the night sky. "Why is it," he murmured, "that wounded warriors feel compelled to minimize their own wounds? With all due respect, Sir Leffingwell, would you send a man into battle with gaping gashes in his shoulder and thigh?"

Leffingwell shifted his great bulk with an impatient grunt, then growled, "Of course not."

"Then why inflict that on yourself?" Jack shrugged.

"Because the King dispatched me to find—"

"You think the King is a more callous commander than you, sir? You think the ruler of us all has less regard for his cherished knights than you do for your own retainers? You are jesting, aren't you?"

The knight grumbled some reply, but Eric couldn't make it out. Maybe that was just as well. Jack turned around and asked cheerfully, "So, Eric, how do you plan to lead us tomorrow?"

"Lead us!" Leffingwell blustered. "You're talking to a boy, trashman! I'm the knight in charge here!"

"I'm talking to Pangbourne, here, not to a boy," Jack responded evenly, his eyes never leaving Eric's. Eric's head reeled. How did Jack know his family name? He'd never shared it, he was certain of that! Jack continued, "And if I'm not mistaken, it's he and his lady friend who saved your thin skin today, not to mention your thick skull."

"Lackin," Sir Leffingwell pronounced sternly, obviously greatly incensed, "I think I can understand now why the King booted you out of his presence. You're intolerable!"

With much noisy effort, the great knight shifted his bulk to his other hip and rolled his face to the fire. He was going to sleep, and he wanted everyone to know it.

Jack still watched Eric's face. "What about it, Eric Pangbourne? Where will you lead us?"

Eric was still stunned. "I—didn't know you knew who I was."

Jack smiled again—but this was a slow, sad smile, one that told Eric he knew far more than Eric realized, and that he understood far more, as well. "I'm Jack Lackin, remember? I know everybody's garbage."

Eric sighed deeply and looked away. "Nobody knows the real truth."

"I do. I know the love your parents had for you and the responsibility they instilled in you—and I know more than that."

"What?" Eric frowned. Jack always seemed to do this to him—invaded his privacy, somehow made him feel, naked.

"I know that they're just as proud of you now as you are ashamed of them."

"I'm not ashamed of my family," Eric responded—but he had to look away as he said it. He wished he were somewhere else. This conversation was making him very uncomfortable. "Where's Winnie," he said suddenly.

"Asleep," Lackin answered, and he laid back and laced his fingers behind his head. "That's where I'm going myself." Jack closed his eyes.

Eric frowned. "Shouldn't someone—keep watch?"

Jack's eyes didn't open as he responded, "You're the leader, Eric. What do you think?"

"I—I don't know."

"I have confidence in you, Eric," Jack said, his voice beginning to slur with sleep. "I'm sure you'll make the right decision." Moments later he was snoring.

Eric wondered what time it was. He must have slept a long time, he decided, for he felt fully awake and alert. Had he slept through most of the night? Was it near dawn? Where were Lucifer's minions?

That did it. No more sleep for him. He stood up and tried to remember where he'd left his sword. He'd last been using it by the fire, cutting strips of blanket. He stepped carefully over Jack Lackin and around Sir Leffingwell, searching the ground for it. He saw Winnie sleeping on the far side of the fire and wondered if she was still angry at him. Then he saw his sword, lying beside her, her hand loosely clasping its shaft. The sight made him smile—Winnie had been guarding the camp. Not that he thought her incapable, oh no. He'd not want to be an enemy when Winnie was swinging a blade in anger. It was just that she looked so peaceful, and innocent, and—pretty—lying there in the firelight, sleeping on her watch. Why had he let her talk him into bringing her out here, exposing her to this danger? He stooped to pull the sword from her grasp. Then he turned his back to the fire to gaze out at the surrounding darkness. He could barely see the silhouettes of the two horses, motionless against the black. Were they, too, asleep? He had no one to talk to and nothing to do. Usually, when he found himself in this situation, he polished armor.

No other thought presented itself, so Eric ambled toward the supplies stacked against the other oak tree. He picked up Wantsalot's helmet and turned it over—something fluttered to the ground beneath it.

Eric frowned and stooped to pick up the fallen object. It was a page of paper—a handwritten note—and Eric's frown deepened. Walking quietly back to the fire, he sat with his back to it and quickly read: "Good lad! I knew you would come in quest of the trumpet, and I desperately need your aid. There are many sides to every story. So many have misunderstood my actions! I have much to tell you, but you MUST come alone! Here's how: Leave before daylight. Take the faster horse and ride north. You will be met and will be led to me. Show this to no one! So MUCH depends upon your loyalty!"

Of the many astonishing things that had happened in the past few days, this was the most shocking. Eric's heart pounded in his chest, and his hands trembled as they quietly folded the letter and tucked it away inside his shirt. Who had placed it in the helmet? When had it been planted there? What kind of help did Wenceslas need that he could provide, and what did he mean by many sides of every story? Eric's thoughts raced even faster than his heart. Was it possible that his knight was not a villain after all? Could it be that he was on quest for the King, and that it simply needed to appear that he had stolen the trumpet? He would be met, the note said—had Wenceslas been secretly organizing a cadre of warriors to enact some great plan for the King? So much depended upon his loyalty.

Eric was nothing if not loyal. He had sworn to uphold the King's law and to support his King's knight. If his master bade him come to him without a word to Winnie or the others, he had to obey—didn't he? Eric stood up and nervously paced away from the campfire. He looked back at the sleeping figures and had to ask himself another question: What bound him to this group? What did he owe them, after all? The fat knight obviously had little regard for him, despite the fact that he'd saved his life today. Jack Lackin was constantly turning up unexpectedly, knowing more about him than Eric cared for anyone to know. Maybe Jack thought he was the leader of this group, but when morning came and Winnie and the knight raised their voices against him, he doubted if he would be the leader of anything. He'd come on this quest for the benefit of Wenceslas, not anyone else, and who knew? Perhaps his aid could provide his master with the resources to do some great thing.

Besides, he thought, as he watched the firelight flicker on Winnie's cheeks, if he left now on Glory, Jack and Winnie would be obliged to put Leffingwell on George and take him back to the city. They'd all be safer there, while he—he would be on a quest authorized by his master.

The decision was made. Eric didn't hesitate. He walked back to the pile of armor and took the scabbard and bound it tightly around his waist. He didn't sheath the sword—not here, where the scrape of metal slipping into metal might wake the sleepers. Rather he carried it with him to Glory's side, took the horse's reins and led her across the meadow toward the north. He walked the horse for what seemed a terribly great distance—far enough away that the fire's light had become but a flickering orange star on the far side of the field. Then he sheathed his sword, climbed up onto Glory's back, and slapped the animal's rump. The black horse leapt out into the equally black night, and Eric rode blindly toward his master's side.

He was thrilled. He was terrified. These two emotions wrestled within him as the horse crashed through unseen bushes and ducked its head beneath invisible low branches. Eric buried his face in Glory's mane, uncertain if the pounding sound he heard was the noise of his steed's flying hooves or his own racing heart. His teeth began to chatter—that was the terror—and then he found himself giggling. That was the thrill.

Eventually he could take no more of either kind of excitement, and he dragged on Glory's reins and slowed the horse to a stop. His new mount was far different from George. It was clear the horse regarded this as merely a brief interruption and waited impatiently for permission to gallop on.

After he and the horse had gotten their breath back, Eric peered ahead into the darkness, trying to make out the dim shapes of something—anything. It was still too dark. He then tuned his ears to listen and heard all kinds of forest night noises—sounds never heard in the city. He mostly heard crickets and frogs, although he couldn't tell them apart. That chirping blanketed all other sounds, muffling any specific noises that might have given him a clue about where they were. The fact was that Eric had no idea where they were, other than in the wilderness someplace. He pushed that thought away, however. He didn't want to think about how far he was from home or about the friends he'd abandoned beside the campfire—or about the dangers he knew lurked in these woods. Eric wanted to think about good things, positive things, that would encourage him and justify what he was doing. "What I need to do first is find Wenceslas," he said aloud. Glory snorted expectantly and took a tentative step forward. "Yes," Eric muttered, "go on," and he flapped the reins—then immediately pulled back on them as the horse seemed to leap again into the darkness. "Slowly!" Eric commanded, and Glory slowed down but didn't stop. Eric sat back and took several deep breaths, trying to relax.

His imagination soon took over his thoughts. He saw himself returning to the city in triumph at his knight's side. His parents were in the crowd, waving to him proudly, and there was nothing in either his father's manner or in his that recalled the estrangement they felt from one another. Winnie was there, smiling proudly, having forgiven him for leaving her with Jack Lackin, now that she understood. All of the other squires lined the streets, some of them cheering, others regarding him with jealousy, wishing it was they and not he who rode up the cobbled streets past the gaily decorated houses of a grateful people. Yes, he, Eric Pangbourne, lowly squire, had ridden out of the city in quest of—

Clunk! He felt the tree limb before he heard it, but it was the crunch the branch made against his forehead that sickened him. Eric managed to cling to the reins as he flipped backwards, twisting his body painfully as he finally tumbled down Glory's right side. He clung to them with both hands as he felt his back smack against the horse's hindquarters and his feet bounce off the ground. Then he had to let them go—it was either that or be dragged under Glory's heels. He called to the horse to stop even as his already damaged face burrowed down through the branches of a bush. It happened so fast he had no time to throw his hands up to protect his face—he hoped his eyes weren't damaged. He immediately pushed himself back up to his feet and hobbled forward a few steps, calling to Glory to come back. Then he fell to his knees and grabbed his head, for the pain of that forehead blow only now grabbed his full attention. Eric groaned—a deep, heartfelt groan which made absolutely no change in the combination of burning and aching pain which suddenly gripped him like a vise. He couldn't remember anything hurting quite so much in his life. He was marginally aware of the scrapes and cuts on his cheeks and neck, as well as the leather burns in his hands and the bruises along his thighs and ribs. But it was his head that complained the loudest, and Eric was quickly realizing why. His fingers were sticky. He couldn't see it in this darkness, but he knew the feel and smell of blood. "Good King," he murmured in shock, "I'm really hurt—" He was also alone in the forest at night, a goodly distance from his friends and without a mount. All those terrifying thoughts he'd previously managed to deny suddenly flooded into his aching head, and Eric trembled. He would have started crying if he hadn't passed out first.

8

IN THE REBEL CAMP

"I think he's coming around," Eric heard someone say.

Someone's found me and I'm going to live! Eric thought, as he silently rejoiced. Then he shifted position. Eric's second thought was, *I wish I were dead!* A terrible ache extended from the top of his head to the ends of his toes.

"Yes, he's awake," said the voice—then it added doubtfully, "I think."

Eric opened his eyes to see who this was. He couldn't open them far, he discovered. They were swollen almost shut, and this effort made them burn with pain. He quickly shut them again. "Oh good King," he murmured, remembering his scratching descent through the bush. Would he ever see again?

"What good king?" said the voice, lightly mocking. "I don't know any good kings, do you?"

"What?" Eric frowned—then he thought better of it. *My face must be scratched to shreds*, he thought. During the days while it was healing, any expression would probably feel terrible.

"I said I don't know any good kings, and I'd be willing to wager everything in your pocket that you've never met one either." The speaker chuckled, and there were several cackles from around him. No, Eric didn't recognize any of these voices.

"I don't make wagers," Eric mumbled, trying to hold his cheeks still as he spoke—that was better.

"Then you've missed out on one of life's finer pleasures. One of you lads go tell the captain that our visitor is awake. I'm Lefty—or so they call me, boy. And your name?"

Eric struggled again to widen his eyes. This time he blinked his way through the initial burning, and they stayed open. Eric was greeted by the sight of a grinning giant. His enormous black beard curled all over his face, so thick and coarse it seemed a more fitting cover for an animal's hide than a man's chin. All Eric could make out through it were Lefty's brilliant teeth. Above a bulbous nose Lefty had brown eyes that seemed to sparkle with mischief—or worse. He really didn't have eyebrows. Rather, he had one single eyebrow extending from one side of his head to the other that was just as shaggy as his beard. Perhaps all the facial hair was to make up for the hair Lefty didn't have on his head. Above that thicket of an eyebrow, the giant was as bald as a rock.

"Your name, boy?" Lefty asked again, not so patiently.

"I'm—" Eric hesitated. This was not because he thought he could hide his identity from these people who had found him, but because now that he could see their faces he felt he knew who they were—and the thought was chilling. He was among brigands, thieves, Lucifer's henchmen.

"Speak up, lad," Lefty said quietly. He smiled a dangerous smile that seemed to threaten some consequence if Eric refused.

"Eric Pangbourne," he answered. He wasn't frightened—or at least so he told himself. He just saw no point in antagonizing such people. "Squire to Sir Wenceslas," he added for clarification.

"Sir Wenceslas!" boomed another voice as the speaker approached, and Eric painfully turned his head to see who was coming. "We were coming to meet you for him! How fortunate for us that we found you! It appears to have been good fortune for you as well."

In the Rebel Camp

A tall man with a thin, angular face and very blue eyes approached them. He was clothed in the raiment of the woods, as were Lefty and the other brigands in Eric's line of sight. The greens, grays and browns they all wore would hide them well in the bushes. "I'm called Hood by the King's knights. Don't know why that might be, unless it's because of the headgear I wear when I slit their throats." He looked about at the others as he said this, expecting laughter—and receiving it. He suddenly reached back to flip a dark green hood over his head and thrust his nose in Eric's face. The hood shrouded from view all but those piercing blue eyes. Eric shivered. He certainly wouldn't want to meet this green-masked marauder in the woods.

The man leaned back, pushed his hood out of the way, and favored Eric with a smile of welcome. "I'm the captain of this merry band," said Hood, laying a hand on Eric's shoulder. "I trust you've been made comfortable?"

"As comfortable as possible, under the circumstances," Eric said, and he shrugged. He immediately wished he hadn't. He wondered if there was a part of his body that wasn't bruised.

"You've taken quite a fall, my boy. From a horse, I assume?"

"Yes."

"We may have collected your mount. Black in color? Highly spirited?"

"That's Glory," Eric said without moving his head. He felt some relief, but just because these people had collected his horse didn't necessarily mean they intended to return it.

"Took you under a branch in the dark, did she?"

"Yes." This drew chuckles from all around him, and even Hood smiled. It made Eric feel like a buffoon, and he wondered if he was blushing.

Hood's expression immediately changed: "Don't be embarrassed about that, boy! It happens to all of us from time to time! It's a natural law that when you ride blind in the darkness you bump your forehead. The trick is to learn how not to fall off. Most people in the city never learn that. They seem to believe there's something or someone about who will always pull the low branches out of their way!"

The troop of brigands chortled at this, and the captain smiled warmly. "You'll learn, Eric Pangbourne. That's not the way things work in the real world. It's an important lesson, and you've the good fortune of learning it early. Are you hungry?"

Eric licked his lips and found them parched. "More thirsty."

"Ah-HAH!" cackled the captain. "There's a lad after my own heart. Lefty! Bring something to slake this night-rider's powerful thirst!" Hood stooped over Eric and looked him in the face. "You've cut yourself up, my boy. May take some days to heal."

"I'll be all right," Eric mumbled, reaching up to touch his forehead. He found it tightly bandaged.

"Of course you're all right. And you'll be more all right soon! Lefty!"

"I'm coming," Lefty snarled, and suddenly Eric felt himself being hoisted into a sitting position. A mug was put to his lips and turned up. He had no choice but to drink—and immediately spewed it out.

"That burns!" he coughed, and the band of marauders laughed again—at least, those who hadn't been sprayed laughed. The others glared at Eric while they wiped themselves off, making no secret of their malice.

"Don't spit it out boy. Drink up!" Hood roared, jerking Eric's head back by the hair as Lefty again tilted the mug forward. This time Eric swallowed it down, even though it made his throat burn worse than the scratches on his face. "More!" the captain ordered, and again the stuff sloshed into his mouth and he swallowed.

Several gulps later he found himself growing woozy. "There now, lad! Feeling better? You keep drinking this elixir and you'll soon feel much better!" It was a good thing the two brigands were holding him up, Eric decided. Otherwise he'd fall backwards, flat on his back. He wondered if he would care—or if he would even notice. His head twirled like a child's pinwheel.

IN THE REBEL CAMP

"Sir Wenceslas?" he asked, trying to get the captain down to business.

"There will be plenty of time to talk of Wenceslas later. Right now, you need to drink up! And if you get hungry, there's plenty of food. We live well here in the forest. Don't we lads?" His words were answered by a weak cheer. The other thieves seemed to have lost interest in this conversation with a boy. As Lefty kept pouring drink after drink down Eric's throat, Eric lost more than interest. He lost consciousness.

When he woke up it took him several minutes to get his bearings. He'd been moved, for now instead of laying on the cold ground he was propped up on pillows in a large circular room. A candle chandelier lit up the walls, which appeared to be moving, almost as if breathing. He was in a tent, a very large tent. It probably would be a very pleasant place to be for someone whose head wasn't trying to split open from the inside. Eric closed his eyes and touched his bandaged forehead. It was sore, still, but he wondered if the burning liquor didn't have more to do with this present pain than his head wound.

He rolled onto his stomach and glanced around. It seemed that every object in this place was either trimmed in gold or accented with red. Eric had time only to think of how tawdry it all appeared before he felt like he was going to be sick. He shouldn't have rolled over—at least not so fast.

"Eric, my boy!" he heard Hood speaking behind him as the man ducked under the flap. "You survived the trip I see."

Eric wanted to tell him that he hadn't quite survived it yet, but he was afraid to open his mouth. He was certain much of his nausea was due to the drink, but some of it was simple fear. This was no dream. He was no longer safe within the walls of the city. He'd abandoned his friends without a word of explanation, and now he was missing Winnie terribly. And he was a captive—he had managed to fall into the hands of Lucifer's rebels, and who knew what they might do to him?

"Why assume we'll do anything to you?" Hood asked, reading his mind. Eric jerked in surprise and looked up at the towering

59

man. "What?" Hood asked. "You're surprised that I read your mind? No great difficulty there, Eric. You display your feelings as prominently upon your face as you do those scratches." Hood tucked his robe under him and folded himself down onto a stool. No longer wearing the garb of an outlaw, he was now gowned as regally as any knight. Hood stroked his bony knees as he leaned his head back and studied the roof of the pavilion. "Right now, for example, you're thinking how lonely you are, and how guilty you feel, and wondering what you'll ever say to the disappointed people you've left behind." Hood looked over at him. "Am I right?"

Eric nodded and swallowed. At least this way he didn't have to talk and run the risk of being sick.

"One sure remedy for what's making you feel ill, Eric. More drink." Eric groaned. "Now, we won't force it down you this time. Before, we just needed you more—pliable—so we could travel here more easily. Where's here?" Hood asked, raising his eyebrows, and Eric nodded that, yes, that had been his thought. "Our camp, of course. Our own city, separated entirely from your 'High City,' totally portable and totally livable." Hood snorted. "You didn't think there was another city, did you, boy? You thought we scurried about in the woods all the time, lurking in dank caves, longing to return to our glorious mountaintop home?"

Hood hooted and stood up to pace about the tent. "We'll return again, Eric, on that you can depend. But not to hang our heads in shame and confess our guilt and bear the scornful gaze of those we've 'disappointed.' We're rebels, lad! Listen to the ring of that word! Rebels. We're free! And we grow stronger every day! One day we'll finally tip the balance, Eric. There will be more of us living in the woods than up there on his mountaintop, and with a mighty shout we'll rush up there and take it back!" Hood was strutting now, his neck stiff, his chest thrown out, his chin jutting arrogantly, those blue eyes mocking. He saw Eric making this judgment and chuckled low in his throat. "Perhaps that day will come sooner than later! What do you

In the Rebel Camp

think, Eric? With one blast from that so-called Archlord's trumpet, will the walls come tumbling down?"

Eric took a deep breath. He'd almost forgotten what he'd come out here for! "You have the trumpet?" he asked.

Hood raised his arms and made a great show of looking up his gown's very full sleeves. "Does it look like I have the trumpet?"

"Your people, I mean," Eric muttered.

"My people? They're your people too, Eric. Don't tell me you're still denying that to yourself?"

"When will I see Wenceslas?" Eric asked in the strongest tone of voice he dared use with this self-described cutthroat.

"When will you admit to yourself your fascination with this place and your curiosity about its pleasures? Stop denying yourself, lad! Until we storm the High City and take back what is rightfully ours, we rebels live very comfortably indeed!" Hood whistled, a shrill, shocking sound that caused Eric to clap his hands over his ears. A moment later people began to pour in the door of the tent and began to party around him—and not just men. His eyes widened, for more than half of the celebrants were women, and they were wearing far less clothing than he was accustomed to seeing females wear. He shot an anxious glance at Hood to find the man watching him—gloating. "You thought we were alone out here? A group of lonely men huddled together for warmth around a poor campfire?" Hood grabbed a bottle out of the hands of a giggling girl and waved it over his head. "Remember how bored you were the other day?" he shouted at Eric above the growing din. *How did he know these things?* Eric asked himself. "Remember how you looked this way and longed to taste life?" Hood pushed his way through the swelling crowd of revelers until he was standing over Eric and thrust the bottle down into the boy's face. "Here, Eric. Taste it."

"I—"

An astonishingly beautiful girl—a woman, really, several years older than Eric and easily the equal in beauty of any lady of the court—sank down on a pillow next to him and took the bottle out of Hood's hand. She turned it up and took a long, sloppy draught, then wiped her red smear of a mouth with the back of her hand and fixed her flirtatious gaze on Eric. When she threw her free arm around his neck and pushed the bottle up to his lips, Eric felt all his muscles going limp. This time no one forced him to drink. He chose to. And as the caustic liquid burned its way down his throat again, Eric was thinking to himself, *She sure beats Lefty!*

9

LEFT BEHIND

Winnie stood at the edge of the meadow and peered northward through the thicket of trees. They'd traced Glory's trail easily to this point—her hooves had churned up great tufts of the grass as she'd picked up speed—but here the trail turned into a tangle. The horse could have gone any direction. With a wounded knight to care for and only one horse between the three of them, she didn't even suggest pursuing Eric. But she wanted to. Once again tears slipped down her cheeks, tears of rage and betrayal.

How could he do such a thing to her? The tears dripped more freely now, but Winnie made no move to wipe them. She deserved the right to feel miserable. "Eric!" she abruptly screamed into the woods. "How could you do this?"

Part of her misery she was doing her best not to admit to herself. If the truth were told, she wondered if she wasn't somehow responsible for everything. After all, she'd been the one who had driven him out here on this insane quest. It had been her idea, as she'd insisted on reminding him. If anything happened to him she guessed it would be her fault. Then she'd gotten angry at him when he hadn't understood her feelings or even seemed the slightest bit interested in them. She'd not talked to him all that last day together. He was a boy, after all. Maybe he couldn't understand. Maybe he just got sick of her. More tears came, and she finally broke down and wiped these away.

"Don't worry," said Jack Lackin. He'd left their patient on the other side of the meadow and walked across it to come up behind her.

Winnie started to whirl around and shout in his face, "What do you know about it? You're just a failed jester!" But she didn't. What good would that do? Instead, she sighed, "I can't help it." She looked Jack in the face, sighed again, and said seriously, "Can you help me understand this?" adding by way of explanation, "After all, you're a man."

"Hmmm," Jack nodded. "I don't know that it has so much to do with being a man as it does being young." He looked at Winnie, the ghost of a smile playing about his lips. "Can you help me understand this? After all, you're young!"

Quite against both her principles and her will, Winnie smiled—but only for a moment. Then her frown settled back down around her face, locking it into a mask of distrust and suspicion. "I sometimes think you know far more than you're willing to say. I don't know if I like that. It seems to me that if you know something that would help us all, you should tell us."

"Something that would help us all," Jack echoed her softly—sadly. "What would help us all? When I was a jester I often found myself saying words I thought would help everyone. But how can you help everyone when not everyone agrees what would be helpful?" Jack peered wistfully into the woods. "One thing I know, Winnie. I cannot control what anyone else chooses to do. I can control what I choose to do. Is that knowledge that would be helpful for everyone? Is it helpful to you?"

Winnie's frown darkened. "Are you saying I shouldn't worry about what Eric does," she snarled, "but ought to concentrate instead on what I do? What about when he does things that affect what I can control—like right now?" She expected Jack to flinch, or backtrack from his words, or something. Instead, Jack's features seemed fixed in stone as he replied:

"I can't tell you what you should or shouldn't feel, Winnie. I'm telling you that you're free, no matter what I, or Eric, or Sir Leffingwell do, or think, or say. You're free to choose how you will respond to life and how you feel about it." He nodded gravely into the woods. "So is Eric."

"Are you sure about that?" Winnie demanded, frustrated that Jack seemed just as incapable of understanding her as anyone. "What if he's been kidnapped?"

"Hmmm," Jack nodded. "I'm almost certain he has been."

Winnie's jaw dropped open and she whirled around to stare at him. "You're certain he's been kidnapped and we're standing here talking about it? I don't understand you, Jack Lackin!" She spun on her heels in the soft grass and marched back across the meadow to their camp.

"No, you don't," she heard the man say softly behind her, but she made no further response. It was her own fault for listening to a jester and a garbage collector!

Everything is my own fault, thought Winnie.

Eric could see it all, but he couldn't believe it. The rebel camp was enormous. Row after row of breathtaking pavilions towered over wide, carpet-covered avenues. People were everywhere, talking, laughing, playing music, dancing, drinking, buying, selling—it was more than he could comprehend. His neck already ached from twisting this way and that to keep from missing anything. No place in the city sparkled like this! At least, no place he'd ever been. He reminded himself that he'd never been within the high towers, and that from below, the walls of the upper city seemed to glisten like crystal.

"Ohhh, look at that!" Lila gushed, tugging on his arm and turning him around. *Talk about crystal,* he thought to himself. "Aren't they gorgeous!" she squealed, pointing to the rows and rows of dazzling crystal objects that dangled from a canopy overhanging the street. Twisting in the sunlight, they reflected a rainbow of radiant color. *Pretty,* Eric mentally agreed. But gorgeous? He would reserve that word for the brunette beauty beside him, who even now was slipping both arms around his waist and nibbling on his ear. "I need one," she was murmuring to him.

"Hmm? What?" he said.

"Buy me one!" Lila's arms cinched him tighter, squeezing his breath out as she plastered her body to his.

"Buy you—" he mumbled. "But I—I don't have any money."

"So?" she cooed, her breath tickling his ears. "There are lots of ways to get money, right?"

Eric was having trouble breathing. Whether it was from the pressure of the arms wrapped around him, or the spicy scent of her perfume, or the clear implication from Lila that somehow he owed her something, Eric didn't know. He guessed it could be all those things at once. Whatever, he needed to squirm his way out of her grip to gasp for air, and he was finding that very difficult to do.

"You could go with Hood," she suggested, walking with him as he stepped backward. She seemed oblivious to the reason for this dance, intent only on hearing herself say, "Hood just takes money away from people."

"Lila," he grunted.

"Or it might be that there's some other way you could help him, and he would maybe pay you for that."

"Lila—"Eric said, his backward steps growing bigger. The woman simply matched her stride to his and went on:

"You may know things he needs to know, or he might could introduce you to people you need to know."

"Lila, I—Ungh!" he grunted, for he'd backed into someone hard. He'd learned already that in the forest that could be dangerous, and he finally jerked himself free and spun around to apologize. He never got the words out of his mouth. Instead he gasped, "Lawrence?""

The older squire was equally shocked. "Eric?" he said, his eyebrows knitting together in obvious fear of being recognized. Lawrence flushed at the same instant Eric realized he was flushing. A moment passed between them while they earnestly searched one another's eyes, realizing what this meeting meant. Although each of them thought it, neither of them actually voiced the question, "What are you doing here?" The moment passed. Their eyes lingered. They made a mute bargain. Then they laughed. As Eric listened to his own laughter, something inside of him mourned, for he recognized immediately where he'd heard this laugh before. It was the laughter of the forest—the haughty, arrogant, derisive laugh of Hood's marauders. In so short a time had he and Lawrence both become brigands?

The thought was squelched. Eric laughed again, more harshly than before, and turned to grin stupidly at Lila. Lawrence glanced down and up the woman and chuckled wickedly. "Not bad, my friend!" he leered, his head bobbing like a barnyard rooster. Then he jerked his head to the blonde on his own arm, and it was Eric's turn to look and leer.

"Not bad yourself," said Eric, copying Lawrence's cocky head-bounce. It seemed the thing to do at the time.

"Do you boys know each other?" Lila asked sweetly, exchanging a knowing gaze with her blonde counterpart. "Why don't we all go back to Hood's place and have a party?"

The idea stunned Eric. Lawrence spoke up quickly, "Oh, I don't know. Becca and me, well—things to see, people to meet. Another time?" Then he was pulling Becca past Lila, shooting Eric one last look. That brief glance conveyed a host of messages: a plea for Eric never to reveal what he'd just seen; a warning that if Eric ever did, Lawrence would pound him into pulp; a slimy leer of wicked excitement; and—strangest of all—a kind of welcome to the fraternity. The look made Eric feel like a co-conspirator—which, he guessed, he must be. It made him feel dirty. Somehow, however, it also made him feel included.

He had only a moment to marvel at this unaccustomed emotion, then Lila was back in his ear, her body once again draped around his. "Of course," she murmured, "we could have a party by ourselves."

"'He'll make the right decision,' did you say?" Sir Leffingwell was barking to Jack Lackin, and with his great girth, when Sir

Leffingwell barked it simply couldn't go unnoticed. At least, Winnie noticed. Jack's mind seemed elsewhere, as if he listened to conversations in a completely different place. "And I suppose this was the right decision?" Sir Leffingwell demanded of the jester. "I think not! He's a runaway! Just like my own squire. Worthless! Useless! His ignorance matched only by his arrogance!"

When Jack didn't respond, Winnie filled the awkward silence. "Do you mean Eric? Or Lawrence?"

"I mean both, girl, and I wasn't talking to you."

Winnie clamped her mouth shut and wrapped her arms around her knees. *Of course not,* she thought to herself in wordless rage. *How could a girl possibly express any worthwhile comment?*

"I understand why they call you 'Lacking Sense!'" the knight announced, fiddling helplessly with the bandage on his thigh.

"Are you thinking we should have chained him to one of the oak trees here?" Jack murmured, his voice seeming just as distant as his thoughts. "Did you happen to bring any chain with you?"

"You shouldn't have encouraged him to believe he was in charge!" Leffingwell snorted. "That put ideas into his head."

"Hmmm," Jack nodded. "Probably so. He may have done what he did for very good reasons."

"I doubt that!"

"The point is, we don't know. Perhaps Eric himself doesn't entirely know. The question for us remains, what do we choose to do about it?"

Sir Leffingwell harrumphed, then planted the palms of his hands on the ground to either side of him. "I'm doing nothing about it. I have my own quest, and it's—" he interrupted himself with a groan as he struggled to push his way up. He failed, then decided to try another way, rolling over to try to climb to his knees. With many more grunts and groans he continued: "It's a quest to—to find—that—that Wantsalot—and to report his—ungh!—location." Kneeling now, the knight replenished his air supply before standing on up.

Winnie looked at Jack and waited for him to tell the knight to lay back down and be still. Instead, Jack responded, "I admire your fortitude. Can I help you in any way?"

"Jack!" Winnie said, almost scolding. Then she closed her mouth again, realizing that it was the burden of this wounded knight that kept them from pursuing Eric. If he was to leave—

"You can get me my armor," Leffingwell muttered, then he looked directly at Winnie and added, "And you can bring me the horse."

"You can't have George," Winnie said without a moment of hesitation. "George belongs to us."

"George, as you call him, is the horse of a King's knight," Leffingwell answered sternly. "I am a King's knight in need, and I claim the animal for the King's use."

"He's yours," Jack said calmly, turning to go fetch the horse from his grazing place in the meadow.

"Lackin!" Winnie shouted, her voice shrill. "You can't give Eric's horse away—he's not yours!"

"He's not yours either—missy," Sir Leffingwell grimaced as he pushed himself all the way to his feet. His tone of voice wasn't harsh or angry. It simply dismissed her opinion as if it was beneath consideration.

"No," she said flatly. "You can't take George."

Suddenly he looked at her, and his expression had changed completely. "Do you expect me to walk to battle, wounded, wearing armor? Who do you think you are, girl?"

"She's the woman who saved your life," Jack said as he led George close to the fire. "Where do you intend to go?" he asked.

Sir Leffingwell seemed a bit startled by the question. "Why—forward, I suppose."

"Seeking some sign of Wenceslas?"

"Certainly."

"Could it be that Eric had some indication of his knight's whereabouts?"

"He didn't know," Winnie broke in. "He only came because he thought I did."

Now Jack turned his even gaze on Winnie. "Do you?" he asked.

She blushed. He waited for her response. "No," she finally managed to get out, and she looked away.

"Perhaps he learned something the other night. Perhaps that's what caused him to leave. Since we've no other trail to follow, could we try to follow Eric's?"

"Of course," Winnie said quickly. It's exactly what she'd wanted to do all along. Jack looked at Leffingwell.

The knight shrugged. "It makes no difference to me. Even if he was taken captive, his trail could still lead us to Wenceslas."

"Then we're agreed," Jack said simply, and he went on about the business of assembling the knight's gear and helping Leffingwell into it.

Winnie watched all of this and wondered. By making himself the servant, how effectively did Lackin lead?

10

LUCIFER'S PAVILION

Eric knew his thinking was cloudy. He knew he ought to take some steps to clear his mind, and he intended to—very soon.

As Lila led him down one carpeted walkway after another through the maze of the mobile city, Eric kept telling himself that very soon he would need to turn his thoughts back to his King and his quest. Yet each time he was about to dismiss the enticements of this place from his mind, Lila would lead him around another corner, and there would be yet another visual delight to distract him.

He couldn't believe the camp was so huge! It seemed to be as big as the city itself! And everywhere he looked people were looking at him—some peering at him suspiciously. Some seemed to dismiss him even as they gazed his way. But most gave him that same characteristic smile that seemed to linger upon the lips of every person here—a smile that seemed to say, "I'd eat you if I could!"

When he glanced over at Lila to comment about this, he saw even she wore that same, chilling smile. Why then, he wondered to himself, did he feel so attracted by it all? For he couldn't deny that he was fascinated.

Hanging on his arm, Lila blinked her long eyelashes at him and bubbled, "Have you seen enough?"

"Enough for what?"

"Enough to want to stay with me, silly!" she said, smiling that smile. "To stay with us." She ran a hand back through her long black hair.

"I—I don't—I don't think that I—"

"Not yet? Ohhh—" she pouted prettily.

"Well hello!" said someone behind them, and they turned around quickly to see that it was Hood. "Eric, lad! Having a good time?" He was putting an arm around Lila's waist and an arm around Eric's as he spoke.

"Yes," Eric nodded, a bit uncertainly.

"Lila, you've been showing him everything?"

"You know better than that, Hood. We've just been at it a few hours! I couldn't begin to show him everything in one morning!"

"No question about that!" said Hood, forcing a chuckle and smiling at Eric. Eric had the strong impression that these two weren't really talking with one another at all, but rather were repeating carefully scripted lines for his benefit. "But, there will be plenty of time for that later, right, Eric?"

He wished he could wiggle out of Hood's embrace. "Ah—"

"Right now, there's someone I know you—ve been dying to meet."

"Wenceslas?" Eric interrupted, suddenly excited again about the real reason that had brought him here.

Hood's grin didn't fade. "Come and see!" he said, releasing Lila and gesturing forward. The woman stepped quickly aside, and Hood pulled Eric forward.

Eric didn't resist. He matched Hood's quick pace as the captain led him down carpeted walkways he and Lila had not yet strolled, switching back and forth at busy intersections so similar that Eric knew he could never find his way out of this place by himself. He and Wenceslas had never been close, but he was very much looking forward at the moment to again seeing his knight. Surely his master would know their way back home.

Eric wouldn't admit to himself his greatest fear—that Sir Wenceslas might be these brigands' captive. To do so would force him to admit to himself that he, too, might be a captive. After all, he'd not tried to leave the camp. Would he be permitted to if he tried? As they threaded their way through the enormous encampment, it became apparent that they were passing successively larger pavilions. Directly ahead of them loomed the largest pavilion of all. From what kind of tree did they hew the tent-post that held this tent up? Who moved it when the tent was raised? How many hundreds of men did it take to hoist the pole into the sky? They headed right for it.

"He's in there?" Eric asked, impressed.

"He is," Hood grinned broadly back, then they were at the tent flaps. These were so large that, were they to be pulled back, they could admit a marching army. The flaps were closed now, guarded by half-a-dozen alert warriors. These checked Hood and Eric for arms, then stepped aside to admit them. Once within the tent Eric found himself in a maze of canvas corridors even more confusing than the streets outside. He was thankful that Hood knew where they were going.

After many twists and turns they suddenly stepped out into a large room, and Eric gasped at the sight. They might be in a tent, but this space was more beautifully decorated than any place he'd seen in his life. Gold glittered upon every wall, illuminated by thousands of burning candles suspended above them on golden chandeliers. His feet sank into red carpet at least an inch thick, and a glance at his feet assured him that golden threads had been woven into the carpet as well. Gossamer curtains, which appeared to Eric to have been woven of spun gold, divided the room into sections. Everything in this pavilion spoke of luxury and opulence. Eric didn't quite know how to react.

"Welcome," said a figure who stepped through the shimmering curtains—and now Eric was truly awed. Dressed in a purple velvet robe which draped from his shoulders to the floor, the splendor of the man was every bit the match for this room. He had long flowing hair more beautifully coiffed than that of any lady of the court, so blonde as to rival the gold decoration in the walls. A beard, equally gold and curly, hung halfway down his chest. His teeth were as ivory white as the marble columns that graced the highest spire of the city, and his eyes were like two perfectly matched emeralds.

Eric was obviously in the presence of a lord of some kind, and he felt compelled to drop to his knees. "No need for that," the purple-clad figure said warmly, but he seemed neither surprised nor bothered by Eric's demeanor. It was as if he accepted this as his due but felt no obligation to force it. "Stand up, my friend," he said, reaching down to help Eric to his feet, then guiding him through the curtains to a sitting area.

Eric sat down in a chair so comfortable that it seemed almost to wrap itself around him. He couldn't help but snuggle down in it, and as he did so he became aware for the first time of the luscious mingling of scents that floated in the air. He drew in a deep breath, sampling the aromas and trying to place them. He could not. Instead he began to feel dizzy, excited and relaxed, all at once.

The gorgeous lord, who had seated himself across from Eric, apparently understood Eric's expression. He smiled and nodded, and gestured for Hood to come and join them. It seemed like several minutes before everyone stopped just smiling at one another and the beautiful man leaned forward to address Eric directly. "I see you got my note."

Eric grinned back at him stupidly. "Note?" he asked.

"Yes!" the golden-haired figure responded. "The note I left in your armor!"

Eric blinked and pursed his lips, and struggled to clear his mind. His head had been cloudy all morning, but this was something different. He felt almost as if he had been drugged, and he felt certain that he ought to feel terrible panic at this moment. He didn't. All he really felt was puzzled. He reached inside his shirt to pull out the note from Sir Wenceslas. "This is the only note I found in my armor," he said. Odd, he thought, how his voice sounded—as if he was talking out of a barrel.

"May I see it?" the gold lord asked politely as he took the paper from Eric's hand and opened it. He smiled again and handed it back. "That's it," he said.

Eric felt terribly puzzled. "But—I thought it was from—Sir Wenceslas," he mumbled, certain that he sounded like a dolt. Somehow he didn't care.

"Who? Who is this Wenceslas?" the golden figure asked, arching an eyebrow.

The panic that he'd known he should feel several moments ago finally arrived in Eric's mind, and it had immediate impact on his body. He began to tremble, although he had the impression he was trembling in slow motion. "Who are you?" he managed to make himself ask.

The beautiful lord's face didn't move, nor did his smile fade. But something in those clear green eyes shifted, and Eric saw the change and shivered. Evil! There was evil here!

"Who do you think I am, Eric?" said the golden prince, bending forward so his face loomed large in Eric's vision. Those eyes cut through him like blades of green light.

"Lu-ci-Lucifer?" he stammered.

"Lucy Lucifer?" the man mocked, again arching his eyebrow. He glanced over at Hood and winked, then those cutting eyes sliced back across Eric. "Lord Lucifer," he corrected in the stern voice of a tutor. "Say it, Eric."

Eric didn't want to, but he did. "Lord Lucifer," he sputtered.

"Very good," Lucifer smiled, moving back to sit deep in his own chair. "You'll become accustomed to saying it, Eric. You'll take pride in saying it."

"But the note—" Eric began.

"Read it again," Lucifer cut him off. He gestured toward the page Eric still clutched in his hand. "Aloud," he added with the unmistakable authority of one who expected always to be obeyed. Eric obeyed. "'Good lad!'" he read. "'I knew you would come in quest of the trumpet, and I desperately need your aid. There are many sides to every story. So many have misunderstood my actions! I have much to tell you, but you MUST come alone! Here's how: Leave before daylight. Take the faster horse and ride north. You will be met and will be led to me. Show this to no one! So MUCH depends upon your loyalty.'"

Eric's eyes rose from the page to see—Lucifer's smile. This was the smile he'd seen everywhere in this camp. This predatory smile was the father of them all. "You see?" Lucifer said. "My letter to you, Eric. All true. You have come in quest of the trumpet. How true it is that there are many sides to any story! You've certainly not heard my side, sequestered as you've been up in that mountaintop fortress! I've been so misunderstood, Eric! Terribly misunderstood! Why, I've been told that some people up there actually think I'm a fire-breathing dragon!"

Lucifer shot a contemptuous look at Hood, who chortled appreciatively. Lucifer looked back at Eric and almost pleaded with him, "Up there they call me a villain, a cutthroat, an outlaw, but I ask you, Eric, when a man strikes a blow for freedom against tyranny, what can the corrupt authorities call him but an outlaw, hmmm? When the laws are unjust and the people oppressed, any courageous warrior who sounds the battle cry of freedom must do it from outside the law! That is what I am, Eric—a freedom-fighter. If I am called a rebel, a guerrilla, by the knights of the King, it is only because I must fight in the only way available to me, using stealth and deceit and all the cunning I can muster. I'm the hunted one, Eric! Put yourself in my place for just one moment. Can't you see how your High City's practice at war must appear to me?"

Eric was struggling to maintain simple consciousness, much less to follow Lucifer's argument. The sweet-smelling smoke that seemed to hang in a cloud in this room robbed him of both the ability and the will to think for himself. "I—I suppose—"

"Of course you can! Anyone can, once they're provided with an unbiased perspective. Naturally I'm accused of making war, but it's only because I must in order to save the freedom of my people! Don't you see, Eric? I let down my guard for just one minute, and your King and his minions scoop us all up and drop us into the darkest of dungeons. Now look at me, Eric. Look around you. Do I look like I should be considered a threat? I live in a tent, for goodness sake! A nice one, true, but a tent just the same. And why? Because I must be ready to move at a moment's notice, to flee to another hiding spot in the forest, oppressed and attacked at every turn by those self-righteous busy-bodies who call themselves 'King's knights.' Oh, how I loathe them, Eric. And you will too."

"I—I don't really know—"

"On the other hand, lad, you might just glance around and see what we poor forest-dwellers have managed to drag together as an abode. You walked through the camp this morning—a part of it. Weren't you just a little bit amazed? Weren't you fascinated by the wealth of creature-comforts, objects of art and feats of engineering? Why, I'd put my people up against the best of the city's specialists in any field, any! The King's people are soft. They've grown fat on no competition, but they've lost their edge, Eric—they've lost their edge. Listen to me, boy!"

"Uhhnn?" Eric said, jerking out of a stupor. It wasn't that he hadn't heard Lucifer's words—it was more that he found himself being hypnotized by them. And there was no question—the golden prince did make some very important points.

"And you know what, lad?" Lucifer snickered, tossing his golden hair back over his shoulder. "You know the best part? There are people on the far edge of my encampment—children mostly—who couldn't care less about that city set on a hill. Some of them don't even know it's there and wouldn't care if they did! The forest is their home and to be cramped up into those straight-laced streets would feel like a prison to them! And yet your Archlord Michael and his storm-troopers comb the forest looking for us, attacking, harassing, massacring my people! I can't let that continue, Eric, now can I? Can I, Hood?" he shouted suddenly at his captain, who quickly chimed in:

"No, my Lord!"

"Can I Eric?"

"No," Eric blurted, terrified by the bulging-eyed rage Lucifer was now displaying to him. He didn't know if he believed what he heard himself saying. It really didn't matter, Eric supposed. In this camp, survival was all-important. He would say what he needed to say to survive, just as it appeared everybody else did.

"Of course I can't! That's why I need something, some edge, some angle, some secret weapon! Something that can help me carry the battle to the city itself! Perhaps—a trumpet?" Lucifer was looking at Eric carefully, his white-teethed smile very broad. "Specifically, that horn Gabriel is always toting around with him on special occasions, but no one has ever heard him play." Lucifer was grinning now as he strolled around the room pretending to play a slide trombone. "Do you ever wonder, Hood, if he even knows how to blow the thing?" Captain Hood laughed appreciatively—and far too hard.

"Why, just think what would happen if the King should finally decide he was too bored to continue, and said, 'Little boy Gabe, come blow your horn! The world's full of sinners and my patience is worn!'—and Gabriel should look at him and say, 'Do you mean I'm supposed to know how to play this thing?'"

With the focus off of him Eric struggled to clear his thoughts. Why was he here? He'd thought that Wenceslas was in the camp, but if Wenceslas was here, wouldn't Lucifer have the trumpet already? A bigger mystery presented itself—what was the horn for, anyway? "What would happen if he did blow it?" Eric murmured.

Lucifer swung his handsome face back around to peer down at Eric. "You really don't know? They don't teach you children like they used to, I see. And how could I possibly object to that! What would happen, what would happen—" Lucifer seemed almost bemused by the question, then he looked at Eric and smiled brightly. "I don't know. I really don't. Would the walls come a tumblin' down? Would the clouds be rolled back as a scroll? Would everybody drop dead or fly up in the air without their clothes on, simply—," he snapped his fingers, "disappear?"

Lucifer shrugged. "Who knows?" Then he eyed Eric closely and let yet another smile blossom slowly across his face. "Wouldn't you like to know? I know I sure would!"

"Me too," Eric mumbled, really not all that aware of what he was saying. Still, at the moment it seemed to be the most enticing mystery one might contemplate. What would happen if a trumpet blast stopped time?

"Listen to that, Hood! He's a man after my own heart. Very well then, lad, it's time."

"Time for what?" Eric asked.

"Time for you to tell us what you know of your master. Time to tell us where he is." Lucifer had sat back down in his chair. He laced his fingers together before his face and tapped his chin with them as he gazed expectantly at Eric.

"What?" Eric asked, wincing. He knew it didn't sound like a terribly bright response, but he really didn't know what else to say.

Lucifer waited a moment, then said, "I think you understood me perfectly. Hood, don't you think he understood?"

"I'm certain of it," Hood replied.

"But—I don't know where he is," Eric said honestly. "That's why I came out here—I was looking for him. That's the only reason I responded to your letter!" he realized suddenly. "Surely you know that I don't know where he is!"

Lucifer thought about that, then scratched his cheek reflectively. "Perhaps—he wanted us to think you didn't know. What about that? Suppose you're a diversion, a cunning gambit designed to lure us into believing you don't know where he is?"

"What?" Eric said again, again wincing.

"Hood, would you step out and find Lefty?"

"Yes, Milord," Hood nodded, grinning slightly. Eric certainly didn't like that grin.

"Now, Eric," Lucifer went on, scooting his chair forward so that he could lean his face across Eric's knees, "this is the way it is. You see, your master was in the camp—and the trumpet too—and we were very pleased by that turn of events. I really can't tell you just how pleased I was. But, it seems he played a little trick on us—with some help, you understand; he didn't do it alone. The outcome being that he and the trumpet disappeared.

"Well, suddenly you show up in the forest, riding Wenceslas's horse, wearing Wenceslas's armor, traveling directly toward us like some utterly blind fool—so what are we to think? That this is all unrelated? That you are simply an empty-headed squire, a sorcerer's apprentice who thinks he can twist the arm of fate and wring from it some glory, perhaps? Sorry, lad, but you must understand I am not much of a believer. I find such a story very hard to believe—especially when I'm told that you travel with some very powerful colleagues."

Eric laughed. He didn't mean to, surely. This was certainly not a laughable situation, what with Lucifer himself sitting across from him and bald-bearded Lefty coming soon to pull his nose off. Still, the idea that a moody scullery maid; a fat, wounded knight without horse, armor or squire; and a garbage-collector constituted a powerful band of co-adventurers simply couldn't be taken seriously. So Eric laughed.

Lucifer frowned at him, at first, but then began to join in, chuckling along with him, and that made Eric laugh harder, until he grabbed his sides and held them to keep them from hurting. While he did so he felt the bulge of Jack Lackin's bell in his pocket, and that stimulated yet another gale of laughter from him, as he tried to gulp out, "A girl, a pompous windbag, and a fool?" He pulled the jinglebell out of his pocket and held it up as he cackled, "Come on now!"

He wasn't prepared at all for Lucifer's response. Suddenly the man was on the far side of the room, seemingly hiding from him behind an armchair. "What's the matter? What happened?"

"I—ah—I quite agree," Lucifer called out rather weakly. "I don't know how I could have gotten such a mistaken notion. You're right, of course. You know nothing. How could you? Why not—put that away, and let's just talk for a few moments about—about your master."

"Wenceslas?" Eric frowned, pocketing the bell. "I don't know if I can tell you anything worthwhile."

"Try me," Lucifer said, sauntering slowly around the armchair. "What are his interests? What does he want out of life? Does he have any hiding places?" Lucifer sat down across from him again and peered at him in a kindly manner.

"Well," Eric said, thinking. He couldn't help but be just a little impressed with himself. After all, here he was sitting with the great rebel himself, and the man seemed to think him important—a "player" in kingdom events. "I guess—the main thing—"

"Here we are, Milord," Hood said as he reentered the room, the enormous, hair-covered Lefty behind him.

"Welcome! Lefty, how are you, my friend? Sit down, grab a drink—our friend Eric is about to fill us in on everything we ever wanted to know about Sir Wenceslas. Go ahead, Eric. Ah—get him a drink, will you Hood?"

"Well, as I started to say," Eric began again as Hood placed something that smelled intoxicating into his hand. For long hours thereafter he told them everything he could remember about his master—his family, his friends, his relationship to his neighbors and to other knights, the foods he liked, the clothes he favored, the ladies he courted, the jokes he laughed at, his strengths in battle, his weaknesses in battle, his art collection, his hunger for possessions. Everything.

He told all this with a gusto born of his new awareness that, to these people anyway, he was more than just a lowly squire. He told all this in a snide tone of voice, making it unmistakable that he really thought very little of Wenceslas. He told it to a very appreciative audience who repeatedly praised his marvelous story-telling skills and urged him to be even more detailed. And as they laughed and joked at Wenceslas's expense, it wasn't very long before Eric felt like he'd known these men forever and that he belonged here.

"Now," chuckled Lucifer, once it seemed they'd drained the subject of Wantsalot completely dry, "Why don't you tell me how you met up with that idiot Lackinsense?"

"Lackin?" Eric said, and he thought about that for a moment—but not critically. There was no thought by this time of withholding any information from his buddies or of somehow trying to protect Lackin from them. It was simply a surface review of his mind as he tried to piece together where to begin—then he was off: "I didn't meet Lackin; he met me. He was always meeting me. In fact, I couldn't get him off my back!" The others roared at this, and Eric laughed along with them, heartily. Then he went on to tell them everything he knew about Jack Lackin, leaving out nothing. As they laughed and teased and bantered back and forth, Eric began to feel a little dizzy and more than a little bit sleepy. He did remember one thing he thought, just before passing out. *Eric*, he'd thought to himself, *you're in. You've finally made it into the club!*

II

ABANDONED

The drizzle on his face woke him. He felt something slick and slimy around him. It was mud, and he was lying in it. To get away from the drizzle he had rolled over and stuck his face down in it. "What?" he said, pulling his nose up out of the muck while trying to clear his breathing. "Unnnyh!" he groaned. Never had his head hurt this terribly! Again he was waking up in a horrible place.

"Where—" he grunted, sliding his knees up under him and struggling up onto them to look around. "What happ—"

The night's events flooded back in on him. He'd spent the evening partying with Lucifer. So where was he now? Eric had an awful taste in his mouth. He rubbed his tongue and looked at his fingers, then immediately wished he hadn't. "Unngh!" he gagged. His mouth was full of mud. He spat and spat, then struggled to his feet and looked around. Mud stretched in every direction—just mud.

He could see trees in the distance, ringing the giant mud-hole, but they all looked equally far away—miles away, he judged. He turned in a slow circle, surveying the emptiness around him and realizing that his first impression hadn't been quite right. There was more than mud here. There was also garbage.

The camp had moved in the night. Lucifer had apparently received that "moment's notice" and had departed, taking his people, their dwellings, and their crystal baubles with them. All they'd left was the garbage—including him.

The conclusion was unmistakable. Eric was garbage. They'd used him up the night before, digging from him the information they'd needed and discarding him like trash. Indignation flushed through him.

"Lucifer, you devil!" he roared at the top of his lungs. "I'm not just some package you can empty out, then wad up and throw away!"

He could see everything clearly this morning, for although his head hurt horribly, it was also clear again. It hurt to think, true, but at least he was able to think. And why had he not been able to think straight since the night he'd left Winnie sleeping by the campfire? Lucifer! He'd been tricked, trapped into revealing all of his master's secrets—and his own, and those of his friends.

His friends. He thought about Winnie and wondered where she was right now. He wondered what she must think of him. He dodged the thought immediately, for he couldn't stand to face what must be the truth.

"It's all that Lucifer's fault!" he grumbled to himself. "He made me do it; he made me tell! And Winnie will understand that, as soon as I tell her. She'll realize just what happened and why."

Eric's stomach was rumbling, and it occurred to him that in the couple of days he'd spent with the rebels he'd really not been given anything of substance to eat. Plenty to drink, he would grant—but food? Now that he thought about it, he couldn't remember a meal, and his stomach was not at all happy about that turn of events. He began to glance around on the ground for something he might eat.

Garbage. Nothing but garbage. Still, there might be something lying around here. Eric picked a direction and started to walk, his eyes on the garbage and the mud.

How could I have been so blind? he thought as he searched. It wasn't that he hadn't been warned of Lucifer's cunning. It wasn't as if anything that had happened in the camp was a real surprise to him. He stopped to flip over a pile of rubbish with his toe—nothing.

He walked on. If he'd stayed with Winnie there would be bread to eat, at least. *Well,* he comforted himself, *no need to panic. I'll find something soon.*

He hated Lucifer. Golden drapes, golden chandeliers, golden lies! He was an absolute and utter liar! Yet his lies were so seductive. The way he wove his lies into the truth while intoxicating the mind and creating diversions for the eye—*why, he was a magician,* Eric thought, *an expert at sleight of hand. It was all Lucifer's fault, all of it. Probably it was Lucifer who'd put Wenceslas up to stealing the trumpet in the first place.*

Wenceslas, Eric thought, wishing he didn't have to. *Where is my master now? How did he get away from the rebel camp? Who helped him?* The next thought stabbed Eric through the heart. *Is my master still free, or has something I said, some bit of information I divulged last night, somehow led to Wenceslas's capture? Does Lucifer have the trumpet now because of something I have done or said?*

Eric stopped walking and sat down in the mud. He put his hands over his head and cowered there for a moment, shaken to his toes by his own embarrassment. He had betrayed his master! He, a sworn squire especially known for his loyalty, had betrayed his own knight! He'd betrayed his friends! Most of all, Eric realized, he'd betrayed himself.

As these thoughts tumbled through his mind, Eric found it difficult to keep his eyes from leaking. Already the back of his throat had started aching. "What have I done?" Eric muttered into his mud-caked lap. "What have I done?"

He would have sat there feeling sorry for himself all day were it not for the fact that he was starving. Had he carried anything to eat with him? He thrust his hands into his pockets and found . . .

The bell. Lackin's bell. That was all he had left, apparently—a stupid little bell from the cap of a jester who was his friend, whom he'd betrayed. And now he couldn't stop it. A tear broke loose and trickled down his cheek.

"Eric!" somebody called from across the muddy field. "Eric! Is that you?"

They'd not even camped the night before, which caused Leffingwell no end of grumbling. "It's *not* a decent way to travel!" he'd groused, making sure both Jack Lackin and Winnie heard him. "There are ways to do things and ways not to do them—rules of order and decency. And this is not a decent way to travel!" Neither had paid any attention to him, intent as they were on pursuing Eric's tracks.

Between George's indifference and Leffingwell's pain, they'd not been able to travel with any great speed. They had, however, moved steadily. They'd found the dead campfire of Hood's marauders. The outlaws had evidently felt very secure, for they hadn't bothered to cover their tracks. When through the drizzle they stepped out of the forest to behold the vast, mud-caked field, they all knew perfectly well what it was.

"This is where they were," Winnie snarled, her anger masking her hopelessness.

"Wh-wh-why did they move?" Leffingwell sputtered, not at all pleased himself. "Why the DEVIL did they move?"

"Simple," said Jack Lackin. "Archlord Michael and the High Host are on the march, and this is not an easily defensible piece of ground. Lucifer's no fool. He always chooses his battle-grounds carefully."

"The mountains, you think?" Leffingwell wondered aloud. "You think he's moving back up to one of his mountain caverns?"

"If that's where Wenceslas went, I'd suppose Lucifer went after him," Jack answered, studying the mud carefully.

"Doesn't make sense," Sir Leffingwell grumbled. "I think he's got Wenceslas already."

"No," Jack said flatly, earning Leffingwell's annoyed frown. "He can't have the trumpet. Not yet. If he had, he would be blowing it by this time."

"Maybe he is and we just can't hear it," said Sir Leffingwell archly. "After all, none of us have ever heard it before. We wouldn't know its sound if we were to hear the thing blown!"

Jack rose up from looking at the mud and looked instead at Leffingwell. "If someone had been trying to blow Gabriel's trumpet, we'd know."

There are many things that Jack just seems to know, Winnie thought. *Who is he, really? It doesn't matter,* she made up her mind. *Whoever Jack is, I will follow him.*

Suddenly Jack seemed to straighten up, and the focus of his eyes went elsewhere. They'd both seen him do it before—it was as if he listened to events in a different place. "Eric," he said suddenly, and his gaze focused on Winnie. "He's here."

"Where?" Winnie demanded, but already Jack had whirled around and was running across the wide field shouting, "Eric! Eric, is that you?"

Eric instantly recognized Jack's voice and immediately turned away from it. He couldn't face Jack and the others—not yet! He felt so terribly humiliated. He'd left their campfire with such good intentions—and such arrogant expectations. How could he stand to tell them the truth? And they would know the truth, he felt sure. Jack, at least, would know.

Eric wheeled around to the other direction and began walking, but his progress was slow—the mud was deep, he was hungry—and for all the fact that he couldn't bear to face these friends he'd abandoned and betrayed, he longed for nothing so much as to be with them again. Still, it was beyond his ability to do what his heart wanted to do—to turn around and run in the direction of Jack's voice. Instead, he had to wait for Jack to catch up to him. Still, he was found! His friends had found him! It wasn't a long wait, after all.

"Eric!" Jack called from just a few feet behind him, and Eric turned around slowly to look at him. Whether from a heightened sense of the drama of the moment or whether he really felt an awful weakness of the knees, Eric fell forward, once more landing on his face in the mud. This time, however, he knew he had friends nearby to help him up.

A moment later, Jack was on one side of him and Winnie on the other, helping him to his feet while an avalanche of questions tumbled over him:

"Where have you been?" "Are you all right?" "Are you hungry?" "Have you been mistreated?" "Why did you disappear?" "Where's Glory?" "Did you meet Lucifer?" "Were you taken captive?" "Have you seen Wenceslas?" "Where have the rebels gone?" "Why did you leave without telling any of us?" "Have you been injured?" "Did they torture you?"

He was relieved there were so many questions. It meant he could pick and choose the one he wanted to answer first. "I was—subjected to—intense interrogation," he admitted as they got him to his feet.

They got under his arms on either side and hoisted him so that he could walk. It was a pretty uncomfortable position, but he obediently moved his legs in concert with theirs, and he had to admit that he made much faster progress across the muck. He looked up in the direction they traveled and winced inwardly. He saw Sir Leffingwell at the edge of the forest, seated on George and looking down on him contemptuously. Well, he'd expected that.

"What kind of interrogation?" asked Winnie. "What were they asking you about?"

"Wenceslas, mostly."

"Then they don't have him yet!" she said across Eric's chest to Jack. "You were right!"

"They did have him," Eric went on, "but he managed to escape. They lured me out of camp to see if I knew where he'd gone."

"They lured you out of camp?" Jack asked simply, and Eric was angry with himself. Why had he volunteered that when he would have preferred to keep it a secret?

"Yes, well—they—they put a note in my armor. They made it seem like a message from Wenceslas. They instructed me to bring Glory and warned me not to tell anyone! I thought I was following my master's instructions."

"Why would Wenceslas send you a note?" Winnie frowned, giving vent to her suspicions. "How would Wenceslas send you a note?" Eric refused to look her way.

"However it happened," said Jack, "you got a note and you thought it was from your master, and he told you not to tell us you were leaving."

"Right," Eric nodded, thankful for Jack's clarification—and for his grace.

Winnie, however, wasn't satisfied. "I can't believe you would pay more attention to some silly note than you would to your friends."

"So you left on Glory," Jack interrupted, rescuing him again. "What happened?"

"I—I got knocked off by a branch in the darkness." Eric pointed to the still-visible gash in his forehead. "That's how I got this."

By this time they had made their way back within hearing distance of Sir Leffingwell, who raised himself up to his full height to look down on Eric and announce, "You've abandoned your post, boy. This will be reported to the authorities when we return home!"

That stung. Eric was about to defend himself when it registered on him that he would have a whole host of misdemeanors to account for, beginning from the day he and Winnie took Wenceslas's horse and armor and rode out of the city under false pretenses. Instead of answering Leffingwell's charge, he just shrugged and continued his story to Winnie and Jack. "I was knocked out. When I woke up I'd been captured by a band of Lucifer's legions. I really had no chance. It was they who had planted the note in my armor and who were watching to take me captive as soon as I left our camp. I played right into their hands," he added bitterly.

"Then why did you go?" Winnie snarled, equally bitter.

"Very irresponsible," Leffingwell tusked.

"I had no choice!" Eric shouted, his anger flaring in self-defense. "I was only trying to do the right thing, and to keep the rest of you out of it!"

"I don't believe you," snapped Winnie.

Leffingwell arched an eyebrow from high on his horse and agreed, "It is a rather incredible story."

Eric jerked his head around to look at Jack. Lackin's response was immediate and unconditional. "I believe every word."

Eric sighed in relief and looked back at the others in the triumph of justification—but they were having none of it. Winnie had come out from under his arm and was walking away, her back turned to him. Leffingwell had already dismissed him and was glancing around them. "This place reeks of evil," he was saying, "but we have found the boy, and we need some rest. Obviously Wenceslas and the trumpet are no longer in this region, but neither are Lucifer's minions. Let's camp."

So, Eric thought to himself, *Leffingwell is now in charge after all*. Well, he could hardly blame anyone but himself. After all, he had left the band.

"I'll get firewood," Winnie grumbled, then added, "if there's any to be found this close to a former campsite." She looked out across the muddy field, wrinkling her nose in disgust.

Eric hadn't intended to speak, yet he heard himself saying, "You should have seen it, Winnie. It seemed to stretch forever, and it was filled with every kind of jewel and joy that anyone could ever want." Winnie turned around to fix him with a gaze so full of contempt that he couldn't stand to meet it.

After staring at him for a moment, her hands propped on her hips, she finally snarled, "Face it, Eric. He seduced you." Then she wandered off into the forest, her eyes intent on the search for firewood.

"Get me down from here!" Leffingwell ordered, and Jack released Eric's arm to go help the knight off the horse. Eric started to help, then held back, wondering if his aid would be needed or appreciated. He didn't want to feel yet another barb from the heavy knight's tongue. Once Leffingwell was firmly planted on the ground beside George, he looked Eric in the eye and said, "The girl's right. I've seen it happen to hundreds."

Once again Eric flared, and he thought of his brief encounter with Leffingwell's squire in the heart of the vain fair. "I've seen it happen to someone you—" he began. He didn't know why he stopped himself, but when he looked again at Jack, the former jester seemed to be nodding in approval.

"Come on, Eric. Let's help Winnie find something to get a fire going."

12

FORGIVENESS

For the next twenty minutes they scoured the forest, and Eric found relief in the activity. Difficult though it was to find worthwhile sticks, it did give him a chance to be alone. Jack searched nearby but seemed content in his own share of the work. Eric appreciated the time to run the experiences of the last few days over in his mind without the threat of public rebuke.

"Jack," Eric called at last, and Lackin turned to make his way toward him. Eric sat down on a short stump, and Jack walked over to sit on the ground beside him.

"Yes?" he asked.

Eric took a deep breath—then faltered. Why was this so hard? It wasn't like Jack didn't know exactly what had happened. *For that matter,* Eric thought, *why do I have to say anything about it at all?*

Jack spoke first. "It might help you to remember that you're not the first person to have been tricked by that liar. You won't be the last, either."

"Ummm," Eric nodded, biting his lip. He still couldn't find a starting place.

"Why not forgive yourself, Eric? I do."

"Forgive myself?" Eric asked. "Me?" This was, indeed, a stunning thought. Eric *never* forgave himself. There was always something more he could have done, some other way he could have or should have managed in any given situation. Failure to find that way simply couldn't be forgiven.

"Why not?" Jack asked. "You're human. Aren't you?"

Eric took a deep breath. "Yes."

"You know what?" Jack continued. "Your father is, too."

His father! Eric never thought about his father if he could help it. His father had become involved in something that Eric just couldn't—

"Let me tell you something about the King," Jack said quietly, and Eric gave his full attention. He'd never heard Jack Lackin speak directly of the King before. "It's a strange thing about the High Court. People here just don't comprehend it at all. Where the King dwells with his archlords there is little talk of failure.

"Listen to me, Eric. Failure can't be judged without being measured against a standard of performance. We have to have a standard to measure our actions against before we can call ourselves a failure or a success. In the High Court there is always and only the best. There is no other standard for comparison. The King's decisions aren't subject to review as 'passing' or 'failing.' He is, after all, the King! Sometimes—it's difficult for dwellers in the High Court to understand what failure really is. With nothing to compare themselves to, how could they ever fall short?

"And then there was Lucifer. Now, Lucifer really had no peer other than Michael. Together they ruled on activities of the court, and no one disputed their choices, nor did they dispute with one another until—"

"Until what?" Eric asked, his forehead creased with fascination.

"Until Lucifer began to compare himself with the King. 'What if I were the King instead of him?' Lucifer reasoned. Now, is that failure?"

Eric blinked. "What do you mean?"

"I'll put it another way. Lucifer was so bright, so beautiful, so magnificent. Well, you've seen him yourself so you understand. He somehow began to see himself as a failure because of the very fact that he wasn't the King—and another was. Do you understand, Eric? He began to judge the Judge. He compared himself to another. He failed. His discontent drove him to rebellion because he couldn't abide his own failure. He still struggles to overwhelm the King because, by his own foolish comparison, the very existence of the King mocks him. It's—sad," Jack said with a quiet sigh.

"But—then—his failure—" Eric paused.

"His comparison of himself to the King became contagious," Jack said. "Others compared themselves to their peers and decided they were failures, too. They rebelled against that feeling with violence, or mocking and seeking to destroy others." Jack looked at Eric and smiled wanly. "It got to be pretty awful."

"You were there, watching all of this?" Eric asked.

"I was there," Jack nodded.

"And what were you doing while all this was going on?"

Jack raised his eyebrows. "I—was—trying to get everyone to—forgive everyone. Forgiveness, you see, was new. This comparison disease was new, and it needed a cure that was equally new. No one had needed to forgive or to be forgiven before all that comparing and judging started to happen. After all this happened, it was needed. Pretty good idea, don't you think?" Jack smiled.

Eric nodded, a bit awed by it all. Then Jack's face fell, and again he grew sad. "Trouble was not everyone wanted to forgive or to be forgiven. Instead, they wanted to be better, to be superior to others, to be 'on top'—whatever that means. And here's the trouble, Eric. You can't forgive and be forgiven and still remain 'on top.' It just won't work."

Jack reached into a pocket and pulled out an apple, red and ripe. "You hungry?" he asked. Eric didn't need a second invitation. He grabbed the fruit and began to devour it. Jack pulled another apple from his pocket and began to munch on it, then he went on. "Unfortunately, Lucifer spread his disease. He began to ask people if they wanted to be little kings. People began to compare themselves to the King and to one another. They began to see themselves as failures and took out their shame and despair on other people, which made them feel less like failures—well, you get the picture. You're living that shame today."

It was the most direct statement about Eric's state of mind that he'd heard, and it rocked him. He blushed—the color of the apple—and he had to stop chewing and take a deep breath. Embarrassed, ashamed, feeling his own failure and feeling anger at being reminded of it, Eric lashed out at Jack, who had been gazing toward the treetops.

"Well what about you? What about what you did that caused you to get booted out of the High City! You feel some shame about that, Jack—don't you?"

Jack turned his eyes to peer directly into Eric's and said, "You see? That's exactly what started happening everywhere. Comparison, a sense of failure, shame, and rage—judgment of someone else. You want to know the truth? It will free you, Eric, if you'll hear it."

Eric stared at Jack, stunned by his passive acceptance of an outrageous personal attack. "Yes," he finally managed to muster.

"Good," Jack nodded. "Actually, I was never kicked out of the High City. It became apparent that if someone didn't start helping people to stop comparing and start forgiving that Lucifer would spoil paradise, not only for himself, but for everyone else as well. I left the High City by choice—to come clean up the garbage.

"Eric, listen to me. You are who you are. You make mistakes and you fail. The King understands. The whole reason I'm here is to tell you that the King forgives you—you and everyone else—even Lawrence."

"You know about Lawrence?" Eric asked.

"I know about Lawrence. I just wish Lawrence knew about Lawrence, like I hope Eric now knows about Eric." Jack Lackin peered earnestly into Eric's eyes, looking for something. Eric wasn't sure what it was. "I'm looking for forgiveness, Eric," said Jack. "Forgiveness for Lawrence, for your father, for old Sir Leffingwell—forgiveness for yourself."

"But," Eric spluttered, struggling to understand all this, "isn't there a penalty to be paid for failure? Some—cost to set it all right again?" Suddenly it gushed out, "Jack, I've betrayed you! I told Lucifer every secret I knew about you, every unkind thing I ever heard said about you! I imitated your voice and I mocked your mannerisms and I—" Eric stopped then, for the tears that had been threatening all morning finally ran free, and there was nothing—not his knight-like reserve, not all the admonitions he'd ever heard that "real men don't cry"—that could keep them from sliding down his cheeks. "I'm sorry," he said at last, but the tears continued. Surprisingly, Jack Lackin met Eric's tears with tears of his own.

"A cost, you say?" Jack answered softly. "Surely this morning you've paid it, Eric, and anything you haven't paid I'll take care of for you."

"But why would you?"

"You've been forgiven, Eric. Let go of all the comparisons and just be forgiven."

"But—the others—Winnie, Sir Leffingwell—"

"Ah," Jack nodded. "That's where it really gets difficult because, as you now know, they want to make you feel guilty. More comparisons, Eric. More of making themselves feel better about their failures by making you feel worse for yours." Jack smiled brilliantly and finished, "More work for me!"

"Eric!" they heard Winnie calling. "Jack! Are you going to let me do all the work?"

"You see?" Jack smiled. "It continues."

"But how do I—"

"Simple," Jack said, standing up and waving for Eric to follow him. "You forgive her, and you do all you can to help. We're coming!" he called. Jack and Eric made their way back to the new campsite. It had been only a few minutes of conversation, and yet somehow, to Eric, it seemed like a lifetime.

The campfire was made, although with great difficulty. The drizzle had returned, and the fire smoked and sputtered in response to the sky's tears. The remaining blankets had been tied to limbs or to poles stuck in the mud, providing at least a little shelter for the drenched band. The only advantage Eric could see to all of this was that it forced them to sit together—if that was an advantage.

Leffingwell slept. While his wounds were healing, he'd lost a lot of strength, and this rough travel was not helping him. Jack, too, seemed to sleep, but Eric had begun to doubt if that was what he was really doing. Was he instead listening to far-off conversations, perhaps even participating in them, while only seeming to be here? Was it possible for Jack Lackin to be several places at once?

As for Winnie, she was still not talking to him. They sat a few feet from one another in dreary silence, watching the fire crackle and spit. Eric was wishing that there was some other way to do this, some means of apologizing without actually having to apologize. He could think of none. Just as he took a deep breath and opened his mouth to speak, Winnie said, "I'm sorry."

Eric jerked his head around to look at her. "You're sorry?"

She was looking away. "It's my fault; I know. If I hadn't brought you out here on this crazy adventure, you'd be safe in the city—I would be there too."

"But, Winnie, it was really—"

"And if I hadn't lost my temper with you for wanting to use my cloth to bandage Leffingwell, we never would have spent that silent day, and I know you would have woke me and told me when you found that note."

"Winnie, none of this is your fault."

"And I'm sorry I was so mean to you when we found you this morning, acting as if I thought you were to blame for everything instead of accepting the blame myself."

"Winnie, listen! It's not your fault!"

"It is too!" she snapped back at him, using the same tone in apologizing as she always did when she was mad. Eric held up his hands and tucked in his chin, his usual defensive posture whenever Winnie was feeling this way. But he couldn't let things rest like this. It simply wasn't true.

"Winnie," he said softly, "listen to me. All right—yes, perhaps you are partly responsible for our being here, doing what we're doing. But—Winnie—" He was seeking for a term of endearment he could use to let her know how much he cared for her, how much he loved her. None came, so he went on. "But I bear all the responsibility for my own actions, and, honestly, some of them were horrible. I was just sitting here trying to figure out how to apologize to you."

She said nothing for a moment, gazing into the fire. "Well?"

"Well what?" Eric asked.

Winnie sighed. "Did you figure out how?"

Eric looked at her, a little smile playing around the corners of his mouth. She was making a point of not looking at him—yet somehow he detected the trace of a grin tugging at her mouth too. *Pretty lips*, Eric thought to himself. Then he realized that, as close as they were under this smelly wet blanket, they weren't really close enough. He scooted over, not daring to look at her. Then he moved his hand down to cover hers. She made no move at first, her eyes fixed on the fire and still sad. Then her index finger popped out from under his hand and onto the top of it. Then she turned her palm up, and they were lacing their fingers together. Winnie looked at him—really looked at him for the first time in a long time. She wasn't smiling, not yet. But she was certainly willing to smile. *What am I supposed to do next?* Eric wondered. Two suggestions popped into his mind. He could tell her, "Winnie, you're my best friend in the world"—which was certainly true. Or he could kiss her. Eric did the right thing. He kissed her.

13

ONE LAST SUPPER

They were all sitting and talking when it happened. It was late in the afternoon. The sky had cleared at last, and the sun had just touched the edge of the western treetops when they were suddenly surrounded.

The High Host had come without a sound. Thousands of them, millions—warriors of the King, whose mirror-like armor glistened pink in the sunset. The muddy plain was covered with them as far as Eric could see. Instinctively, he twisted his head to look at the forest behind him. They were there too—beside every tree, behind every bush, in every direction he looked.

The King's riders—each was mounted on a horse of purest white, and each stood as still as a statue. And though there was not a trace of malice on their faces, Eric was utterly overwhelmed by the power he beheld. They were grim-visaged and sober, unmistakably warlike figures. Yet, Eric saw in their combined expressions not a hint of that selfish blood-lust present in every smile he'd seen in Lucifer's encampment.

But why hadn't he heard them coming? How could an army this vast arrive without a single sound? Leffingwell must have wondered, too, for he leapt to his feet, ignoring the shooting pain in his thigh, then just as swiftly dropped to his knees.

Eric glanced at Winnie and saw on her face the same look he guessed was on his own. They'd spent the afternoon holding hands. Now he felt the pressure of her fingernails as well.

And there was Jack Lackin. The garbageman—how long was Eric going to be able to continue thinking of him as a garbageman?—uncoiled slowly from his seat on the ground and stepped out from under the blanket to gaze westward.

Eric followed his eyes and saw now that the ranks of warriors were dividing in perfect formation, making a lane to allow a small cadre of warriors to ride toward the fire. And though he'd never seen him before in his life, Eric knew without question who the lead rider was: General Michael, the archlord of the Host of the High Court and Lucifer's arch-foe in the field.

What was most striking to Eric was how much the two enemies resembled each other! From Michael's glistening helmet spilled hair the same golden shade as Lucifer's. A curling beard of the same spun gold fell across most of his mirror-bright breastplate. The high cheekbones were the same, as was the thin, straight nose and the arching eyebrows. The only difference Eric could tell was in the eyes—Lucifer's had been a jealous green, and Michael's eyes were as blue as the sky.

Then, suddenly, they weren't. They were, instead, very brown—a rich, coffee brown that Eric found both warm and forbidding. Eric blinked. The warrior he stared up at was no longer blond at all. He had straight black hair that hung to his shoulders, no beard, and skin the color of rust. Even as Eric stared at the man's cheeks, they changed color once again, deepening past rust to a dark chocolate, as the width of his nose and his lips flared wide. Once again he was bearded, but now his curls were tight and black. Then they disappeared again, for his skin had turned a sallow, almost parchment gray, and his hair, though still black, had straightened. His eyes turned black and lengthened into the shape of an almond.

Eric stared. Then Winnie murmured weakly, "Did you see that?" Eric could only manage a grunt in response. Why did—? And then it came to him.

His own ideal warrior was a blue-eyed blond. But what of other lads his age, who lived on the far side of the mountain from his own narrow street? Did they envision the ideal warrior of the High City to look something like—themselves? Michael's eyes met his, and Eric wanted to disappear. Yet there was something in that fierce gaze that said to him, "Yes, lad, you've understood."

The Archlord straightened in his saddle and addressed the tiny band in a voice so deep it seemed to rattle the makeshift tent-poles. "We had a report that the enemy was camped upon this spot. Do you know which way they might have traveled?"

Assuming the question had been addressed to him, Leffingwell stammered for a moment but couldn't find words to say. The truth was, this was the first time the heavy knight had seen the Host of the High City assembled, and he was as awed as Winnie and Eric.

Jack spoke up. "Someone suggested they may have moved northward toward the mountains, but don't take that for the truth. We really don't know."

Michael peered down at Jack from high on his horse, and Eric puzzled over exactly what the warrior's expression might mean. It could be contempt, or it could be warning, or it could be a veiled, ironic smile. Whatever its meaning, it didn't last long before Michael pulled down that same mask of sober, grim preparedness that every other rider in this vast company wore. A moment later, they were gone.

Everyone stood still, as if frozen by this visitation. Then Winnie, Eric and Leffingwell all began to jabber at once, each checking what the others had seen, assuring themselves that Michael had, indeed, changed form at least a half-dozen times during the brief encounter.

Jack, however, took no part in the conversation. He slipped to his place on the ground, tucked his arms around his knees and gazed into the fire, deep in thought. The others quickly noticed his absence and returned to their places, excitedly asking him what he thought of the High Host's appearing.

Instead of answering, he reached into his knapsack and pulled out a bundle containing a loaf of bread and a bottle. "Isn't anyone else hungry?" he asked. "I'm starved."

Before long they were eating supper together—a very quiet supper indeed. The others respected Jack's privacy. No one asked again for his reactions, although Eric felt certain that Winnie and Sir Leffingwell were just as curious about Jack's relationship to Michael as he was. By the time the food was eaten, the sun had set, and after supper Jack got up and began to pace across the churned field of mud. He was looking at the stars, sweeping his vision from one horizon to the other. Eric thought he must be in conversation with someone, somewhere.

Abruptly Jack returned to the fireside and sat down. His face had regained that relaxed, composed look that Eric had grown accustomed to, and the young squire breathed a sigh of relief. His anxiety level soared again immediately, however, when Jack leaned forward into the fire and announced, "We've got to make plans for battle."

"Battle?" Winnie said.

"Battle?" Eric echoed her. Leffingwell struggled to his feet and started for his sword.

"Your sword won't do us much good, I'm afraid," Jack called, and Leffingwell turned to look back at him.

"Not that kind of battle?" the knight said, seeming to understand.

Jack nodded. "Not this time." Leffingwell limped slowly back to the fire circle and gingerly lowered his body into place. "You're still too weak to wield a sword much, my friend. And you, Eric, you're well trained but lack experience. Winnie? To tell you the truth, Winnie, I'd hate to be on the other side of any battle with you, for your will and your courage are like iron! Even so, you haven't the arm strength of a single one of Lucifer's cutthroats. And me? Well, I'm nothing but a fool."

"No—" Eric began, but Jack quickly cut him off.

"Listen to me, all of you. We are the weakest of all the King's warriors in the forest tonight, and that's why Lucifer will drive the battle over us. We could count up our strengths together, but we already know our strengths. It's our infirmities we need to count on, and it's our weaknesses we need to face. I've already told you mine. I'm a fool, a believer in the best during the worst of times, a jokester in the midst of chaos. I have the knowledge of eternity, yet I can also die. And you?"

Jack looked around the circle, touching on each set of eyes, expectantly. There was throat-clearing and foot-shuffling before anyone responded. Leffingwell spoke first.

"I am—well, how do I put this delicately. No, I don't need to put it delicately, do I? Very well. I am fat." He harrumphed some before he could continue. "I know I'm fat. No one needs to point this out to me. And it makes me slow; I realize that. And, strangely enough, I realize it makes me act pompous around people, as if by acting superior to them I can convince them that gluttony is a virtue. There. I've said it." He sat back from the fire, folded his hands across his large belly, and waited for the two young people to speak.

Winnie spoke next. "I am—selfish. Now there are reasons that I could tell you, good reasons, causes from my growing up that would probably make anyone a little selfish and stingy and controlling of others—" Winnie stopped herself, glanced around at the other three, then dropped her eyes and her voice. "But you don't need to know the reasons, do you? You just need to hear the truth. That's it. Eric?"

It had come around to him. What should he say? The truth, of course. "I am—ambitious. I really want to be somebody, someone important, grand, beloved of all. Lucifer played on that somewhere across that field in a grandiose pavilion lined with gold. He fooled me into feeling proud of myself, into expressing that cockiness, that arrogance always under the surface in me. He made me feel like a big man and got me to trade away my self-respect in exchange." Eric sighed, then he shrugged. "That's who I am."

Eric looked across at Jack and saw him staring into the fire. The flames were reflecting in his eyes as he murmured, "Here we are then, a band of the King's people who are fat, selfish, arrogant fools." Jack's eyes flicked up out of the fire and slipped around to each of the other three. "Now the question becomes just how is the King going to use our weaknesses to accomplish His purpose?"

He rolled over to stretch out on his side and said, "That may sound a little hopeless. Does it?" They each mumbled some form of agreement, and Jack nodded. "We'd all better get some sleep. We'll need it. But let me point out that we do still have one thing in our favor." The others peered at him earnestly, and it occurred to Eric in that moment that there was no longer any question in any of their minds who led them now. It was the servant who'd come along to help.

"And that is?" Leffingwell asked.

"Somehow, Sir Wenceslas has managed to keep the trumpet out of the hands of Lucifer. We must take courage in that. But unless we are each faithful, that might not be the case by morning. Good night." Jack laid himself out next to the fire, and in moments he was still.

Sir Leffingwell watched Jack sleep for a moment, then he turned to look at Eric. "One question, lad, if I may ask?"

"Go ahead."

"When you were in the camp of the enemy, did you by chance see the squire assigned to me?"

Eric hesitated. Should he tell? The mute bargain he and Lawrence had made in the enemy's camp had been based on a Lucifer's smile—on an exchange of sordid secrets. Was that binding upon him now?

"Never mind," Leffingwell said, waving the question off. "If he was, I'm afraid I'm as responsible for his being there as Wenceslas is responsible for you. Never mind."

"Sir Leffingwell," Eric said evenly, "I don't blame Wenceslas for my mistakes. Neither should Lawrence blame you. In any case, you certainly shouldn't blame yourself."

"Ah, but that's just it, lad; I do." The overweight knight began to lower himself toward the ground to get some sleep.

It was Winnie who spoke up, who voiced Eric's own feelings better than he could himself. "You know, there's one thing I think I've learned from all this. I think—" She bit her lip reflectively, then finished, "I think we all do just about as well as we can do, under the circumstances. Jack Lackin says the King forgives us. I wonder why we have such trouble forgiving ourselves?"

Did Leffingwell hear? If so, he made no response. Eric did, however, reaching out to take Winnie's hand and squeeze it. They scooted closer together again. "I don't think I'm going to be able to sleep," she whispered, trying to keep the tremble out of her voice.

"Me either," Eric answered.

"Will you just—hold me until it comes?"

At that moment, Eric could think of nothing that would do him more honor. He hugged her to him, kissed her forehead, and waited.

Within moments they slept.

14

THE DARKEST HOUR

They did hear this army coming. They felt it first—a low, rolling thunder coming from under the earth. It woke them all at almost the same instant, and a moment later, they were scattered over the camp, making preparations. Winnie rolled blankets and stuffed them into sacks. Eric ran to unhobble George and to soothe him, for he heard the rumble too and he recognized it as war. Sir Leffingwell bandaged his thigh and got to his feet, then, with the help of Jack Lackin, struggled to get his armor on as quickly as possible.

By the time the bags were packed and Eric had led George into the firelight, Jack was hooking the last clasps that held Sir Leffingwell's breastplate in place. Although their individual tasks had never been verbally agreed upon, they moved with the grace and speed of a trained team. By the time Sir Leffingwell donned his impressive headgear, the huge chestnut warhorse was standing ready beside him, and Jack and Eric boosted him into the saddle. Sir Leffingwell wheeled George around to face the on-coming thunder of thousands of hooves, and the horse reared and whinnied as he set himself in place for the charge.

Eric looked at Jack, and Jack at Eric. "My—Wenceslas's armor?" Eric asked, and Jack nodded toward Winnie, who was already bringing it. Now, as George stamped and snorted beside them, Winnie and Jack did for Eric what Eric and Jack had just done for Leffingwell. Winnie's hands began to fumble as her breaths grew shorter. It sounded like the whole world was riding down on them, and what were they in the face of it? Jack's hands, however, moved with the calm control they always had when collecting garbage. Eric looked up at Jack's face and felt a shock run through him. Jack looked like Michael had this afternoon. His grim, sober expression mirrored every face of the Host of the High City.

"The army," Eric murmured. "Lucifer's?"

Jack nodded curtly, finished buckling on Eric's sword, then without looking up he said, "Look far out to the east. What do you see?"

Eric followed the instructions and saw a dim radiance over the distant eastern trees. "A glow," he answered.

"Now look to the far west."

Eric turned his head and saw the same kind of dim glow. "What is it?"

"Those are the flanks of the High Host." Jack pointed east and said, "They're fanned out in a crescent behind Lucifer's horde, from that point . . . ," he said as he brought his hand across in front of them to point to the western glow, ". . . to that point. If we were to be here to watch it, in a moment the whole northern sky will light up."

"But—we won't?" Winnie asked tentatively, and Jack looked at her.

His eyes were full of compassion as he answered her, "The entire army of Lucifer's rebellion is between the four of us and the Host. And riding for his life before Lucifer comes—"

"Heeeeelp!" they heard in the distance before them, and Jack never had time to finish his sentence. "HEEEEELLLLPPP MEEEEEEEE!" the rider shouted again, clearly riding at them at a full gallop.

Eric knew the voice immediately, for he'd heard it hollering for him and at him many times before. "Wenceslas," he mumbled, more to himself than anyone else. A moment later Sir Wenceslas, mounted on Endeavor, swooped into the firelight and reined the coal-black stallion in. "I need help! Help me! Help me please!"

"Wenceslas?" Sir Leffingwell called out in his most booming, challenging voice, "On authority of the King I demand you return the Trumpet of Do—"

Before he got his sentence out, Wenceslas shouted, "Squire! Eric! Is that you?" He spurred Endeavor's sides so the warhorse sprang directly toward the fire, by-passing George and sweeping between Winnie and Eric.

He wheeled around at Eric's back and screamed, "Why are you wearing my armor?" Then before Eric could answer he shouted again, "Wonderful! Sensible! Climb up behind me!" Then he was over Eric, looking down at him as he extended a forearm. He clearly expected Eric to grab hold and swing onto Endeavor behind him.

"Eric!" Winnie cried.

"Winnie!" he shouted back at her, but Endeavor was too tall for him to see over.

Wenceslas had leaned over and was screaming in his ear, "Get up here, boy! NOW!"

The knight's saddle horn was at eye-level to him, and when Eric glanced down, he saw it—tied up in a black velvet bag, dangling from that saddle, was an object that could only be a trumpet. The purpose of his quest was a foot away from his face. "I SAID CLIMB ON!" Wenceslas shrieked, his face red, even in the darkness. Eric grabbed the extended forearm and swung up into the saddle behind him.

"Eric, no!" Winnie was crying, but he was on, and already Endeavor was springing forward at the prick of the knight's spurs.

By this time Leffingwell had gotten George turned around to face the fire, and once again his voice boomed out, "I command you, Wenceslas, in the name of the King and of all the High Host, that you surrender immediately the Trumpet of Doom."

Eric heard his voice trailing off behind him, for they were already bounding out of the campsite and onto the muddy plain. Despite the horse's screams of protest, Wenceslas continued to rake Endeavor's black flanks with his spurs. He guided the horse in an arc across the field, back southwest and into the woods. "The Spindle," Eric could hear Sir Wenceslas muttering. "We have to make it to the Spindle!"

Eric reached his arms around his knight's waist to grab the pommel of the saddle and to make sure the bag still hung suspended there. The knight's head swerved back over his shoulder, and he spat in Eric's ear, "You touch that bag, boy, and I'll slit your throat!"

Eric closed his hands on the saddle horn and left them there, then he ducked his head down and hid it behind Wenceslas's back. They were riding under trees in the dead of night, and painful experience had taught him what that could lead to. If a branch caught Wenceslas, he knew what he would grab onto in the tumble.

"Why did he do that?" Winnie was shrieking. "Why did he DO that? Why did he GO?"

"Because he had to," Jack said firmly. "He saw the trumpet and he saw the chance. He had to go, and so do you, Leffingwell!"

Sir Leffingwell was having a terrible time trying to get George turned back around to follow Endeavor. George was confused. He was never a nimble horse in any circumstance. He was certainly not accustomed to carrying the weight of a fully armed Sir Leffingwell!

Jack and Winnie raced to George's side, and a moment later still more was added to his burden, as Jack swung Winnie up into the saddle behind the bulky knight. It was unlike George to protest, but this was too much, and he whinnied in complaint. Jack stepped around to seize the horse's muzzle and spoke into George's brown eyes. "I'm sorry, old boy, but do you think you can carry these two for just a little ways?"

George snorted. Whether he understood or not, Winnie couldn't tell, but the horse did manage to step around in response to Leffingwell's urging until it faced the southwest.

"What about you?" Winnie shouted back at Jack, but he just shrugged.

"I don't think old George could manage three of us. Do you?" Lucifer's army was almost upon them. Already they could hear the crashing of trees and bushes to the east. "Do you know the way to the Spindle?" Jack called, and Leffingwell gave a curt nod. "That's where he's going. Ride to him!" With that Jack slapped George across the rump, and the great horse bounded forward. He could hear the pounding hooves behind him. He knew there was little time to pick up speed. The big warhorse ran like he'd never run in his life.

Winnie caught one last glimpse of Jack Lackin in the firelight. Alone, unarmed, he'd turned to face the mounted figures that came bounding into the clearing. Then it was Winnie's turn to crash through the underbrush and under the trees in the blackness. She couldn't remember a darker night in her life. And behind her, still, the Dark One's army galloped. She reached as far around Leffingwell's great belly as she could and buried her face against his back. She pressed her left cheek painfully into the links of chain-mail, and wept at her loss of Eric, of Jack—of herself.

The Spindle, Eric thought to himself. *Where is the Spindle?* He'd heard of it. Perhaps he'd even had it pointed out to him from somewhere along the city's battlements. It was attached to an outcropping of rock that some said looked like a spinning wheel. Supposedly the granite hill jutted up high and thin and round, like a circle on edge. The narrow spire of the rock they called "the Spindle" was actually a cluster of flat-topped spires at the end of the granite ridge. Was it close? Eric supposed it must be. He hoped it must be, for Endeavor now carried the two of them and their armor, and the stallion was obviously flagging beneath them.

The Darkest Hour

"When we reach the rock, boy, you take my back and protect me as I climb! It's our only chance, lad. We've got to get up that rock! It's the only place we can defend ourselves against this howling mob!" Wenceslas's voice cracked as he added, "if indeed we can defend that!"

"Why not surrender the trumpet to the Archlord Michael?"

"Give it back?" Wenceslas raged. "Return it to Gabriel and the High City? And just what do you think they would do to me then, lad, hmmm? They'd hang me in a cage from the tallest spire in the city. They'd leave me there to starve while the people threw refuse up at me and called me names! I'll never surrender the trumpet to Michael, never!"

"But if the Dark One should get it—"

"Then we're all doomed! Oh, I tried to barter with him for it, I admit it, but he just laughed at me. He laughed! He promised me everything—promised me I would be his second-in-command, a pavilion the equal of his own, riches, and women, and works of art. But he lied, Eric! That devil is a liar!"

Eric needed no lesson on that fact. He was confused, however. "But why didn't he just take it from you?"

"Because I set it up perfectly, that's why! I threatened to destroy it! I met him two nights ago in a blacksmith's forge in the heart of the village country. I made him come in disguise, then I held the trumpet over the forge while we bargained. He promised me everything—everything! That's how I knew," the knight finished bitterly.

"Knew what?"

"That he was lying. Eric, lad, there's been no bigger fool in the history of the kingdom than the knight you ride behind. I know that now! But not even I am so big a fool as to believe Lucifer would trade away all his power for a horn. If he'd promised me something believable, Eric, I would probably have fallen for it. What he promised was simply too good to be true!"

Endeavor stumbled under them, then righted himself and continued on. Still, there was no question the horse had almost run his last. "A little farther," Wenceslas pleaded with the animal, almost wheedling—as if he was bartering still.

"But once you knew that, how did you get away?"

"I had help. That's all I can tell you."

"Help from whom?"

"From a garbageman. Now that's all I'm going to say!"

"Jack Lackin helped you?"

"Please, Endeavor," Wenceslas cooed in the struggling animal's ear. He was running gallantly onward, but his whole body seemed to twist with every stride. "We're going down!" Wenceslas whined, leaning back in frustration and almost knocking Eric from the saddle. "No, wait! Look!" He was pointing, and Eric pulled himself up to look over the knight's shoulder. They'd suddenly run clear of the treeline. Looming before them, still blacker than the pitch-black sky, was a wheel-like mountain of stone. "We made it!" Wenceslas shouted in exultation, just as they went head over heels. Endeavor had crumpled beneath them.

Eric realized a moment too late that he should have grabbed for the velvet bag. Instead he grabbed at nothing and resigned himself to another painful tumble to the ground. Surprisingly, this time it didn't hurt all that much. No, not surprisingly. This time he was wearing armor. He skidded for several feet and came up coughing, for his shoulder-plates plowed up a puff of dust. Then he was being jerked onto his feet by his master, who was shouting at him, "Get out your sword, boy, and guard my back! Come on!"

Wenceslas raced off toward the looming darkness, and Eric obediently drew his sword and chased after, following more by the sound of clanking armor than by sight. The other, more oppressive sound in the night was the army of Lucifer, still bearing down behind them. Wenceslas began clanking upward instead of forward, and Eric felt the incline and the rocks around him. He paused and looked back, listening. He felt certain Endeavor had dropped dead beneath them, for he could no longer hear that courageous animal's labored breathing. And

Winnie? And Jack? And Sir Leffingwell? Where were they now? Lost in this tragic night?

"UP HERE!" Wenceslas screamed down at him.

Eric started climbing. But he was thinking better of it. "We can't see where we're going! What's the point of getting here if we fall off the mountain?"

"What's the point of getting here if they catch us at its base? Get up here, Eric! NOW!"

Eric climbed.

Somewhere along the way, without her really knowing when, Winnie's trickling tears had turned to broken-hearted sobbing. As stalwart George plowed forward, Sir Leffingwell evidently felt her heaving through his mail. "Hang on, Milady," he called back, and she could hear his voice rumble through his back.

Milady? she thought. *Milady. Has anyone ever before called me Milady?* It was her dream, of course—what she longed for—to be a lady of the court instead of a maid of the kitchen. And yet, what an odd, impossible place to hear herself called such! Winnie felt like anything but a lady. Oh, she still had her cloth, all seven yards of it. Ever since Eric had nearly used it to stop Leffingwell's bleeding, she'd worn it in a knapsack slung around her neck and under her arm. She'd slept on Eric's chest with it on, even dreamed of wearing it, fully made up as a gown, while walking on Eric's arm. *Lady Winnifred and Sir Eric Pangbourne,* she thought now—once again the tears gushed onto her cheeks.

"Hang on tight, dear lady," Sir Leffingwell tried again, a hint of desperation in his voice. He was a master of offering challenges and exchanging manly banter. But while he knew it was a part of the expectation placed upon a King's knight, he'd never been particularly good at offering consolation. "You've not lost the lad—not yet. We'll be at the Spindle before long. Take courage!" Beyond that he could really think of nothing more to say, so he closed his mouth and concentrated on his riding.

And when we get there, what? Winnie was thinking. Suppose they did catch up with Eric and Wenceslas—were they then to turn in battle array, just the four of them, and hold off that black tide she'd just watched roll Jack Lackin under? She set her jaw glumly and hunkered down against Leffingwell's back. She felt anything but comforted. She grumbled to herself, then she noticed she had, indeed, stopped weeping. Her grief had passed. She was beginning to feel resignation.

The higher they went, the more accustomed Eric became to climbing in the dark. It was slower, of course, than climbing by sight. He had to feel for every hand- and foot-hold and wave his hands in front of him to be certain he didn't slam nose-first into a rock. Still, he liked it far better than night riding. Here, at least, he controlled his destiny. He looked to see how high above the ground they'd climbed but couldn't even see his own feet. He also wondered if getting down from this rock might not be far more terrifying than getting on it, but by this time Eric figured his chances of surviving the night were slim indeed.

The rock was flattening out before him, curving away so sharply he could almost stand straight up. A moment after making this discovery he bumped into Wenceslas, who snarled at him, "Watch out!"

Eric *did* back away a step, but backing away any farther here on the rock was not appealing. "Are we on top?"

"We are," the knight growled. "We need to get across to the Spindle, but we'll have to have light to do that."

Eric sat down where he was and took a deep breath. He thrust his hands back behind him and propped himself up, then scanned the horizon to the northeast. As Jack Lackin had promised, the entire sky glowed. "You think Michael will arrive in time to save us?" he wondered aloud.

"Why do you keep talking about Michael?" Wenceslas snapped. "The Archlord of the Army is in his bed somewhere up in the High City—if they ever sleep up there."

Such bitterness, Eric reflected. He guessed Wenceslas had always spoken to him with that bitter edge in his voice, as if he was always just a sentence away from a tirade. That threat of rage had often prevented Eric from arguing with the knight, even when he knew he was right. It didn't prevent him now. "No, he's not," he said flatly. "He's out there where that glow is, fanned out behind Lucifer."

Eric couldn't see Wenceslas's incredulous expression, but he could hear it. "What glow? What are you talking about?"

"Out there to the northeast," Eric pointed, then he put his arm back down, realizing the knight couldn't see where it was pointing anyway. "That pinkish-orange glow."

"I don't see any glow! Are you trying to make me think I'm crazy?"

Bitterness and suspicion—both seemed always to be present in the knight's tone. "I'm not trying to make you think anything," Eric said wearily. "If you can't see it there must be a reason."

"Can't see what?" Wenceslas demanded. Eric changed the subject.

"Why did you do it?" he asked. He said it so simply and directly that the knight was caught off guard. His reply was uncharacteristically gentle.

"I don't know. It was a spur of the moment thing. All the King's knights were meeting at the entry gate to the High City, and Gabriel had come down to address us. I'd always thought the trumpet was stored somewhere inside a cabinet in the High City, but he had it with him. It seems he always carries it with him, to be ready should the King order him to blow it.

"I watched him stride around the room, so high and mighty, talking about our defense of the lower city, and the thought just popped into my head. 'Why him and not me?' He put it down on the table and walked away from it, and I—I just—picked it up. I didn't mean to take it! You can't think I planned any of this, do you?"

"From what you said, it sounded like you planned out the meeting with Lucifer."

"Once I'd taken it I had to do that! Self-protection, of course. After I'd gotten out of the city with it, I seriously thought about just getting rid of it, throwing it into a lake or something. When

I realized I'd been discovered, I knew it was too late for that. By the time I met with the Dark One, I had already come to grips with the fact that my life was over. I was just trying to salvage something out of the whole episode—enough to get by while I lived out my days in disguise. Oh, Eric, Eric. The act of one moment! One moment! And my life is over!"

"Maybe not," Eric responded hopefully, but it was a weak hope. Chances were that both their lives were over. They could hear the sound of Lucifer's riders encircling the base of the mountain. Eric found the silence that followed ever more threatening. Then from somewhere directly below them they heard Lucifer speak:

"Sir Wenceslas! I believe you have something for me. Do you not? Throw down the trumpet and we'll leave! If not, we'll come up to get it ourselves and throw you down."

As Lucifer was speaking Eric could hear Wenceslas wrestling with something—the velvet bag, he guessed. Then the knight shouted to Lucifer, "If your people place one foot on this mountain I'll blow it! I swear to you I'll blow it!"

Lucifer's laughter drifted up. "What do you think I want it for? To enshrine it somewhere in my pavilion? Go ahead and blow! I want to see what happens!"

"He's lying," Eric muttered under his breath. "He's terrified of what will happen, fearful that the sound of that thing will trumpet the death of his rebellion."

"I know that," Wenceslas grunted back, but he sounded uncertain of himself.

"He wants to control it," Eric argued. "He hates the idea of Gabriel holding his destiny in his hands!"

"You'll have to come and get it, Lucifer. But I promise you, I will see what a blast on it does before you take me!"

"They're coming," Eric murmured, his voice filled with wonder, for the light that spanned the northeast horizon was now becoming a ring that wrapped all the way back behind the mountain. Perhaps Lucifer did have them encircled—but Michael encircled Lucifer.

"Who's coming?" Wenceslas whispered frantically. "Where? Behind us? Some cutthroats?"

"Below us. The High Host. You mean you still can't see it?"

"I don't know what you—," the knight cut himself off with a gasp. At that same moment a scream of terror went up from the brigands at the base of the mountain, and Eric understood, at last, why Lucifer's army had charged on so arrogantly with the High Host on its heels. Until this moment neither they nor Wenceslas had been able to see what was perfectly clear to him. "Would you look at that?" said Sir Wenceslas, enraptured by the sight.

"I have been," Eric shrugged, feeling just a little bit cocky. He was thinking he just might make it down from this big rock after all.

"That's what you meant by—Michael?" asked the knight. Eric heard the fear in the man's voice, but when Winnie shouted at him he was completely distracted.

"Eric!" she called out. "Are you up here?"

She was up on the summit with him! Forgetting for a moment both Wenceslas and his own safety, he hurried across the curving rock in the direction of her voice shouting, "Winnie! Winnie! Here!"

He could see now, at least a little, for the orange-pink glow from below gave an eerie illumination to the mountaintop. He saw her silhouetted against it and rushed to grab her. They rocked dangerously in one another's arms, then crouched down to flatten themselves on the rock's surface. "Winnie! You're all right!"

"And you are too!" They clung to each other, only dimly aware of the battle that had begun all around them.

Soon it was an unavoidable din: clashing swords, screaming horses, shouted battle cries and shrieks of pain. It came from every side of the giant rock as Michael tightened the noose on Lucifer, and the rebels responded in rage.

They drew hope from that—and drew more hope from yet another source of light. A touch of the dawn streaked the eastern sky, and they knew it would not be long before the events of this darkest night stood exposed to the light of day.

15

JACK'S JUMP

"Where's Leffingwell?" Eric suddenly worried, and Winnie shrugged in his arms.

"He started up the rock behind me, but he couldn't keep up. From the way he was talking I don't think he likes rock climbing." She twisted around to look over her shoulder, down the way she'd come up. "I don't see him. He may have gone back down into the fight."

"And Jack? Where's Jack?"

Winnie looked back around at him and took a breath. Her hesitation was answer enough. "Oh, NO!" Eric mourned, and all of the joys of the last few moments suddenly turned again to grief.

"It all happened so quickly," she murmured, remembering her last view of the trashman standing his ground before the campfire. "I didn't actually see him—" She couldn't bring herself to finish the statement.

"There's hope in that, at least," Eric said grimly, getting to his knees to get a better vantage on the battlefield. The noise level grew as still more warriors of each army squared off in individual encounters. There were no battle lines anymore, just a single general melee that stretched as far as he could see in every direction—and he could see farther with every passing minute. Winnie got up on her knees beside him, and they clung onto one another and gazed down in relative safety. Eric kept a vigilant watch all around them, scanning the base of the rock to insure that no one climbed up behind them. As the light increased he could make out far more detail and suddenly climbed from his knees to his feet.

"What is it?" Winnie asked, clutching him.

"Leffingwell. He's in trouble."

The heavy knight had apparently not made it far up the hill before being engaged by two forest-clad brigands. He was giving better than he got, sweeping them before him with scythe-like slashes of his sword, but his wounds still hobbled him. Without help it would only be a matter of time before they took him down. Heedless of the steep incline, Eric plunged down the hillside, his sword in hand. By the time he noticed Winnie was right behind him, it was too late to warn her. For the first time in his life he was at war.

The brigand he reached first never even saw him. Eric slashed his blade through the man's shoulder, then shoved him out into mid-air. He screamed as he dropped the twenty feet to the ground below, but Eric didn't see him hit. He'd already turned to face Leffingwell's other attacker—this man had seen him. Sparks flew as their swords clashed, and Eric felt a jolt through his arms like nothing he remembered from practice. The second jolt was just as hard—the third even harder. This brigand was fighting for his life, and he was far more experienced in battle. Eric felt a brief shock of fear as he realized that he wouldn't be able to parry a fourth blow. Then the danger was just as suddenly past. Leffingwell swept the outlaw from the mountain with a single powerful stroke.

"Help me get him up the hill!" Winnie shouted to Eric, jumping down to Leffingwell's level and ducking under his arm. Now that they were once again above the fray, Eric sheathed his sword and dropped down to help her. With their urging and assistance Sir Leffingwell learned he could climb this rock pile after all.

"You have Wenceslas?" Leffingwell asked, puffing. "You have the trumpet?"

"Wenceslas is right up—" Eric stopped in mid-gesture. He'd pointed to the far end of the wheel-like rock's summit, but even as he did so he realized he had not seen Wenceslas since before the dawn. The three looked at one another in panic, then all turned in unison to the Spindle—the spires of rock that jutted beyond that far end. Wenceslas was on top of the tallest spire.

"How did he get there?" Winnie asked as they hurried along the ridge in that direction.

"He jumped," Leffingwell said, still huffing and puffing. "He had to. The only way he could get over to it is to run and jump and grab hold of that little platform for dear life. The trouble is that there's no way back."

As they arrived at the sharp cliff, all of Leffingwell's words became self-evident. Wenceslas wasn't more than twelve feet from them, but there was room for only one person. They couldn't get out to him, and there was certainly no way he could jump back across that breach flat-footed. He was trapped. Apparently, however, he'd not yet realized just how desperate his situation was, for he was laughing.

"You want this, Lucifer?" he was shouting, waving the trumpet over his head. "You, Michael? You want it? Come and get it! Climb up here and take it!"

Eric stepped to the edge and looked over, and his breath caught in his throat. The other sides of this rock were gentle slopes by comparison. This was a sheer drop to instant death. Eric instinctively leaped back, then got on his belly to crawl toward the edge and look down.

The Spindle was obviously the focal point of the battle. Lucifer had clustered the heart of his army around it and now defended it fiercely, while Eric could see Michael himself mounting just as fierce an attack. The sun had climbed high enough to bathe the battlefield in sunlight. Once again the armor of the High Host glistened pink and silver, and Eric wondered how anyone could muster the courage to raise a sword against such an awesome sight.

Lucifer, however, wasn't even watching. Eric saw him at last, his gaze turned casually toward Wenceslas. "I think you would rather just throw it down to me, wouldn't you?" he called, his voice chillingly polite.

"Now you're dreaming!" the knight roared back, his face twisted into a grotesque mockery of itself.

"Shoot him down," Lucifer murmured, loudly enough for Eric to hear, and suddenly crossbow bolts were whizzing up the cliff-face.

"Drop! Get down!" Eric shouted back at Winnie and Leffingwell, and they flopped on their bellies as the sharp-tipped missiles flew past them. Eric raised his head to see that Wenceslas, too, was flat on his face. A second flight of arrows flew upward, and now he crawled up to his knees, squeezing himself into a little ball with the trumpet clutched to his heart. He no longer seemed to be laughing.

"Keep firing until you knock him down," Lucifer told the captain of his crossbows. "Turn him into a pin-cushion if you like. Just be sure I get that trumpet." Then the Dark One drew his own sword, climbed back onto the steed they were holding for him, and drove through the ranks of his own men toward Michael.

Is this it? Eric wondered. *The Last Battle?* He guessed that depended on what happened to the trumpet. He looked back across the chasm at Wenceslas, expecting to see the man put it to his lips and blow. Instead, he beheld one of the strangest sights he had witnessed in a week of incredible events. Wenceslas had turned his back on the battle and his face toward them. He wedged the Trumpet of Doom between his knees, and between his thumb and his index finger he clutched a jinglebell—a twin of the bell in Eric's own pocket. The knight was jingling the bell with tiny jerking movements and shouting, "Help! Jack! Help!"

Eric was stunned. Quickly he thought back over what Jack had told him when he'd given him his own bell—"Let it remind you that you have a friend who believes in you." Obviously, despite all the terrible things that might be thought and said about Sir Wenceslas, the knight had that same friend believing in him! Eric remembered now. Hadn't Wenceslas told him that it was Jack who'd rescued him from Lucifer the first time? One other thing suddenly occurred to him. Every time he'd rung his own bell, Jack Lackin had put in an appearance! Could it be that—

"Jack!" he heard Winnie shout behind him, and he smiled in satisfaction. Yes, it could. He rolled up from the edge of the cliff to look up into Jack's face and saw exactly what he'd expected: a common, smiling garbageman, clad in the clothes of a peasant.

"Jack," he grinned. "How did you get here?"

"Why on horseback, of course. I caught a ride with Lawrence here." He jerked a thumb over his shoulder, and Eric craned his neck to see that Lawrence was, indeed, standing behind him. The older squire wore a sheepish expression, one that clearly proclaimed there was an embarrassing tale behind all this, and he hoped no one would ask to hear it.

Eric hadn't the time. He rolled back onto his stomach and pointed at Wenceslas. "I think he's calling for you." At that moment another flight of arrows thumped up from below, and this time the bowmen had changed their angle. A crossbow bolt caught Wenceslas in the shoulder, knocking him from his precarious perch.

The Spindle was not really a single spire, but rather three spires of varying heights. Wenceslas had the good luck to drop onto the lowest of the three. It, too, had a flat top, just big enough for a man to kneel on. Wenceslas wedged his body against the taller spires, clung tightly to the trumpet—and wept. Below them, Eric could see the Dark One's bowmen changing their firing angle once again. Now he was even closer.

"We have to do something!" Eric snapped, his voice crisp with authority. "Wenceslas! Throw us the trumpet!"

The man's eyes flew open, and he looked up at Eric with hatred. "Never! I'll never give this up!"

"Sir Wenceslas, listen! It isn't you they want. It's that trumpet! Throw it up to us and they'll stop shooting at you!" *And start shooting at us,* Eric thought ruefully. But with Michael's army surrounding them they would at least have a fighting chance of defending it. Wenceslas had none.

"And then what happens to me?" the knight shouted back, his voice cracking with an almost childish rage. "You leave me hanging here to die!"

"No, we won't. We'll—we'll—get you down somehow," Eric trailed off. The truth was, he really hadn't thought that far. Now he did. "We're going to have to go out there and save him," he rolled over and said to Jack.

"How?" Jack asked.

It was such a simple, guileless question. Eric wished he knew an answer. "If we had any rope," he began, but Jack cut him off quickly with, "We don't."

That was true. Eric chewed his lip. Another flight of arrows whooshed by and clattered off the rocks around the knight. Wenceslas wailed in terror.

"If you had a rope, what would you do with it?" Winnie asked, her voice oddly colorless.

"Well, ah—I could tie it around my waist and jump across to the top spire. Jack could hold it, and Leffingwell could anchor it with his—weight." Eric was afraid to look back at the heavy knight, but there was no need to worry.

"How nice to hear my gut finally getting the appreciation it deserves!" the big man cackled.

"Then I could lower myself down to where he is," Eric continued, "get him to hold onto me, and then swing over to this cliff face. Then the rest of you could pull us up. If we had any rope."

From the knapsack she'd kept tied around her neck for days, Winnie began to pull out her yards of beautiful green brocade. "It isn't rope, but will this do?"

Eric studied her face. It was solemn, and her lower lip trembled slightly—but her offer was real. "Let's try it," Eric said, and he clambered to his feet and reached out to take the cloth.

"No." Jack caught his arm in one hand and with the other he began to tug on the yards of fabric. His relaxed smile was gone, replaced by that same expression of grim resolve Eric had come to expect from King's warriors under fire. "He called for my help—remember?"

Eric looked at Jack for a moment, studying his eyes and remembering that campfire conversation—had it been just the night before? Winnie was being unselfish, Leffingwell was tying one end of the fabric around his great girth, and now it was Eric's turn to—step aside? To stand aside and watch while others did what he dreamed of doing? He glanced again over the cliff and saw that the bowmen were scrambling around, changing positions once again. "You'll never survive," he mumbled, as much to himself as to Jack.

While he'd been thinking, Jack had been tying, and before Eric could say another word, Jack was backing away from the edge—then running toward it. The cloth furled out behind him like a huge green ribbon as he leapt spread-eagle across the chasm and landed safely on the platform. Then, nimble as a chimney sweep, he hopped off of that one to the one below it and was about five feet above Sir Wenceslas's crouching form. The knight turned his red-rimmed eyes up to look at him, and Eric heard Jack say softly, "You're going to have to grab hold of me with both hands, my friend. You just can't do it with that trumpet in your hands."

Wenceslas peered up at him weakly, his hands fumbling with the instrument feverishly. Suddenly he'd made his decision. He shot up to his feet, thrust the trumpet into Jack's outstretched hands, then gripped the garbageman's ankles, clinging for his life. Jack didn't hesitate a moment. He stood, looked up at Eric, and tossed the ancient instrument toward him.

Eric didn't have time to think about catching it. It was arching upward, then it was dropping toward his hands, and he grabbed it. He held the Trumpet of Doom.

Jack wouldn't let Wenceslas cling to him. Instead he grabbed the man's wrists with his own powerful hands and pried them off his ankles. Then he hoisted the knight into the air as a father might lift a two-year-old, releasing him only to catch him again around the waist.

"Jack!" Winnie shouted. "Crossbows! Swing across now!"

But Jack was not swinging across with Wenceslas held in his arms. Instead he untied his long green sash and knotted it around the knight's waist. "You'd never hold us both!" he shouted by way of explanation. "NOW!" he yelled, and he pushed Wenceslas off the edge.

"Nooo!" the man screamed as he sailed out into the air. But the green cloth held, and after the knight bounced twice off of the cliff below them, he got the idea and turned his feet to the rock wall.

"Leffingwell! Everyone! Pull!" Eric shouted, and they all grabbed onto the long green ribbon and backed away from the cliff. The material frayed and ravelled as it rasped up over the sharp edge, and Eric ached a bit inside for Winnie. He would buy her more, he promised himself, if they ever got off this hilltop in one piece. Out of the corner of his eye he saw Lucifer's minions beginning to scramble up toward them—no, toward him.

Wenceslas's face came up over the edge, red as a beat, and with a last powerful heave they pulled him over. "Quickly!" Eric shouted, rushing up to the gasping knight to tear the cloth from around him. "We're coming, Jack!" he shouted without looking down. "We'll throw this back to you and you catch it!"

But when he finally had the end free in his hands and rushed to the edge to throw it over, Jack was gone from the spindle. "Jack?" he called. Then he peeked over the edge and shouted in horror, "Jack! Jack, NO!"

The garbageman's body, pierced full of arrows, dropped into a sea of Lucifer's angry warriors. They began to chop at him wildly with swords and axes and pikestaves. Eric watched in disbelief as Jack's body disappeared under a tumultuous surge of frenzied, flailing outlaws.

Eric stood frozen there on the cliff. It was Winnie who grabbed him and pulled him up the ridge and away. Almost as an afterthought he reached down to pick up the trumpet he'd tossed aside while struggling to free the fabric from Wenceslas. He looked down at it and shook his head. All the tragedy, all the terror—over this.

"Eric," said Winnie quietly, leaning toward him. It was her warning tone, and he didn't even look up from the trumpet. He just drew his sword and made ready to defend the ancient instrument against all of the Dark One's hordes. "Eric!" she said again, more insistently, and now she was also tugging on his arm. He looked up.

16

King's Knight

A moment ago Eric had seen black-clad warriors and outlaws climbing this rock on every side. Now, instead, Archlord Michael stood before him, composed, controlled—victorious? Awed though he was by this legendary figure who stood before him, Eric couldn't help but glance around in concern. Where was the enemy? Why this sudden pause in the fighting?

The answer was apparent. The tide had swung dramatically, at the very moment Jack had dropped into that ravenous mob of human wolves. Lucifer was nowhere to be seen. His minions were sprinting into the woods on all sides, pursued by the silvery knights of the highest court. The rebellion had been checked once again—if not broken entirely. And the trumpet? The trumpet was still in his hands.

He looked back at Michael, who towered over him, and gulped. He wondered if the Archlord ever smiled. Then again, maybe that was a smile, and he just couldn't recognize it.

Another figure stepped forward on the Archlord's right, and Eric gulped again, for he was just as magnificent as Michael.

"Gabriel?" he asked.

The giant nodded slightly and smiled. "I am indeed Gabriel, archminister of the High City who waits upon the will of the King. And you, sir, have recovered something that the King long ago entrusted into my care."

It took a moment for Eric to get the point. When he did, he blurted out, "Here!" and shoved the trumpet forward.

Gabriel took it from him carefully, turned it over in his giant hands as if examining it for damage, then said, "The whole of the realm will thank you."

Eric blinked and said, "No need to thank me. I just caught it. It was Jack Lackin who got him to give it up."

"Nevertheless," Gabriel said, "it was you who, as you say, caught it. And it is you, Sir Pangbourne, who has surrendered it back to me without hesitation."

"Well, after all, it does belong to—" Eric paused. "Sir Pangbourne?"

Gabriel stepped aside, and once again Michael loomed above him. "That sword you hold," said the Archlord, pointing down at Eric's other hand. "May I use it?"

Eric had forgotten he'd even drawn it. He turned it pommel up and passed it over without a word.

"Will you kneel?" Michael said, and Eric sank downward, aware of the band that clustered behind him—Leffingwell to his left, Winnie to his right, behind him Lawrence and Wenceslas. Not until they touched the rock did he realize his knees were shaking.

Then, what he had dreamed as a boy would one day happen, he felt the flat of the blade touch him once on each shoulder and then again on the first. "By direct command of the King himself, I dub thee King's Knight Sir Eric Pangbourne. Rise, Sir Knight, and prepare to ride with us to the High City. The King has asked you to dinner!"

Eric got shakily to his feet and allowed Sir Leffingwell and Winnie to help him down from the rock. What a moment! It had been everything he had ever dreamed it might be—with one exception. He wished his father had been here to see it.

No, two exceptions, he thought sadly. He wished Jack had been here too.

The return to the city was incredibly swift. He thought Glory was a fast horse, but these beasts the Host of the High City traveled upon were simply not ordinary horses! They were greeted by a city that seemed to rock with celebration. In fact, Eric was embarrassed by all the attention, and he began to wonder why he had wanted this.

The High Host didn't pause in the lower circles of the city, but rode furiously upward, scattering unwary citizens unprepared for their sudden ascent. Without a glance, they passed the stables where Eric had served—he was going higher.

When they swept into the High City itself, there were servants everywhere, scurrying about to meet their every need. Eric found this attention equally embarrassing, especially when he was hustled off his horse and into a bathing chamber and stripped of his garments without so much as a hello.

Bathed, shampooed, and anointed with oil, he was guided into another chamber and robed in white silk. Before he had a chance to look at himself, they were strapping pieces of armor onto him—not the working kind of armor worn in the field, but ceremonial armor, delicately carved of silver plate and ornamented with gold filigree. And it was his size! Eric felt a little dizzy just looking down at it—or was it the smell of that oil they'd dumped in his hair? At last they strapped on a sword—again, ceremonial and much longer than the one he'd used that morning. He warned himself to be careful not to trip over it. What an impression to make on the King—to fall sprawling on his face when he tried to bow!

Two servants escorted him through the castle. Still more rooms, more chambers, more enormous, vaulted ceilings. Now Eric realized just how pale Lucifer's pavilion had actually been in comparison. He sniffed the sumptuous aromas from the kitchen and realized how hungry he was! Then they led him into the banquet hall.

He froze in the entryway. If there were words to describe this place, he'd not yet learned them. Words need some image behind them to have meaning—something, he remembered Jack saying, to compare them to. What he saw here moved beyond anything he'd ever seen. He blinked, then looked at the table.

"Winnie!" he shouted.

"Lady Winnifred," the servant on his right whispered in his ear, and he knew immediately this was right. She was radiantly beautiful tonight, and he could tell by her smile that she knew it! What made it most satisfying was the gown they'd robed her in for the evening. Green brocade, yards and yards of it, had been fashioned into the most beautiful dress he'd ever seen.

"Lady Winnifred," he repeated, grinning broadly. "You look gorgeous!" Winnie's only response was a bright, pink blush and a smile.

His eyes ran down the table to Sir Leffingwell, who wasn't looking his way at all. Eric understood. The man was surrounded by every possible wonderful thing to eat! And there, on the other side of Winnie, were his mother—and father.

His parents. He loved them so much. And at that moment he felt shame course through him, for he couldn't comprehend why he had ever been embarrassed to be his father's son!

"Hello, Mother," he said quietly. She beamed at him, then turned her eyes to his father. He followed her gaze. "Hello, Father."

The eyes that looked back into his were filled with such love and pride and forgiveness that he felt like he'd been bathed all over again. "Hello, Son," his father whispered powerfully, then he reached all the way across the table to grab him and hug his head. "I'm so proud of you," he whispered in Eric's ear.

"I'm proud of you too," Eric managed to murmur before a hush swept over the vast banquet hall.

"The King!" someone nearby was whispering, and several people were pointing. Eric twisted around to look over his own shoulder to get his first glimpse of the one he'd longed to serve all his life. An arm slipped around his neck from behind and hugged him, then turned him around and stepped back at arm's length. "Well done, Eric!" he said. "Or rather, Sir Eric. Well done!"

"Jack?" Eric murmured. "Jack?" He was both surprised and not surprised, but he was terribly, joyfully relieved. "Jack!" he shouted, and he hugged the garbageman. Or jester.

Or King? He stepped back and looked at Jack closely, his eyebrows knitting on his forehead. Over his arm Jack Lackin had draped a serving towel—but on his head he wore the crown of the King. "What are you?" Eric said at last, and Jack Lackin threw back his head and laughed.

Then he looked at Eric lovingly and said, "I'm a friend who believes in you and who always will—as I know you, Eric, believe in me. Sometimes I'm still a jester. And, of course," he pointed up to his head, "yes, I am the King."

"My King," Eric said in a whisper, all the breath going out of him as he dropped to his knees before his true Master. "My Lord and King!"

As he'd earlier seen Jack do with Wenceslas, Eric felt himself being hoisted bodily back onto his feet. "Stand up, Sir Pangbourne! Tonight you're the guest of honor, and it's my turn to wait tables. Tomorrow night we'll change places. All right?"

Eric gasped then shrugged, and said, "All right." Then a thought sprang to mind, and he added, "Am I going to have to polish the serving plates?"

Jack laughed aloud at that and slipped his arm again around Eric's neck to lead him to the honored place at the head table. As they walked he was whispering in Eric's ear, and by the time Eric slipped into his chair, he was cackling aloud. That Jack. He told the most marvelous jokes!